UTAH!

SELECTED SHORT STORIES

SCOTTY V. CASPER

IUNIVERSE, INC.
NEW YORK   BLOOMINGTON

UTAH! Selected Short Stories

iUniverse books may be ordered through booksellers or by contacting:

iUniverse
1663 Liberty Drive
Bloomington, IN 47403
www.iuniverse.com
1-800-Authors (1-800-288-4677)

ISBN: 978-1-4401-4252-9 (pbk)
ISBN: 978-1-4401-4253-6 (ebk)

Printed in the United States of America

iUniverse rev. date: 6/5/2009

This is an anthology by a single author and the stories are set in Utah. These stories are in random order, but they bridge an era beginning around World War I to the present. The challenges and difficulties endured by the fictional characters in this anthology closely approximate what real live Utahans have endured in making Utah what it is today: vibrant ... progressive ... up-and-coming. Yes, Utah truly is the Beehive State.

CONTENTS

PLACEMENT

My name is Pat Garley. I was born into a devoutly religious Latter-day Saints family in Oakley, Utah. I was an only child. During this long-ago time, Ike Eisenhower was president of the United States and the country was slowly healing from World War II. I was only a few weeks old when I was carried to the front of a Sacrament Meeting for the obligatory blessing. The Bishop of the Oakley LDS Church, a proud member of the Melchisedec Priesthood and the one responsible for the temporal and spiritual well-being of me, placed his hand on my head, as did my father and the First Counselor. The Bishop offered a prayer to the lord and savior and christened me Patrick Victor Garley—and that's the name I'll carry with me until I go to my eternal reward, whatever that might be.

After the christening I was raised on a strict diet of theology and American values. I was taught to believe in baseball, Old Glory, Chevrolet, and the girl next door. Moreover, my family and peers worked hard teaching me that the Church of Jesus Christ of Latter Day Saints was the only true church. My friends and relatives meant well and I really can't take issue with their gentle urgings.

Taking it further, I am certain that America is great, and, likewise, one can do much worse than follow the LDS church's sensible teachings. In fact, the church is so moral and narrowly restricted in its views that it forbids coffee, tobacco, or alcoholic spirits. The church contends that one's body is a tabernacle and should be treated as such. Regardless, none of it seemed to take hold with me. I just faked it, hoping to make my family and peers believe I was solidly rooted in Mormon fundamentals.

But here's the thing. Much to my chagrin, I discovered I had shortcomings—an evil streak and an ungovernable temper. Case in point, I remember being in an LDS Sunday School Class when I was eight years old. On that day, Sister Benchley, an elderly woman who was God-awful homely and so uptight a D-8 Cat couldn't have pulled a sewing needle out her rectum, taught us the story of Jonah, who was swallowed by a whale. Many of the things the church taught seemed plausible, but somebody being swallowed by a whale and escaping to tell about it? It seemed like a crock. Anyway, when the class was over we were running around on the front lawn, playing tag, and Stan Henderson tagged me, making me it. How dare he? I threw him on the ground and kicked the living shit out of him. This took place back in 1955, before anger management classes were in existence—not that I believe such psychobabble bullshit would have helped me.

That night when we sat down to supper I could tell that Mom and Dad were upset. Dad cleared his throat and I knew I was in for it. Dad was over six feet tall and his body consisted mostly of muscle and sinew. He owned and operated a sawmill and I suppose handling a cant hook each day, and pulling huge levers, and off-bearing heavy slabs, had turned his body into chiseled perfection. Couple his great strength with his temper and that meant trouble to anyone who crossed him. "Before we offer a blessing and enjoy this bounty provided by the Lord," he said, "I'd like Pat to join me in the basement by the laundry chute."

Wherein he took his razor strap to me. He had fetched it from the bathroom before he went down to the basement. It cracked with explosive power when it hit my legs and behind. I bolted for the steps, but before I could get away, he grabbed me and pulled me back toward the laundry chute and slapped me a terrific blow across the face. "Stand and take it, you evil little bastard," he said.

I stood and took it—ten more swings of the razor strap. When it was over I lay crumpled on the floor, sobbing and screaming in agony. The whipping had hurt and scared me so bad that I wet myself. I stripped off my wet jeans and underwear and tossed them in the laundry washing machine. I replaced the wet clothing with soiled jeans and underwear from the laundry chute:

I couldn't go up to dinner in wet jeans. It hurt like a sunuvabitch. Those places where the razor strap struck felt as if somebody had seared me with a blowtorch.

Before I went back upstairs I pulled my trousers back down to look at the damage. I backed up to a full-length mirror and got a good view. I had large welts on my legs and behind. In a couple places the skin was broken and blood was oozing from the wounds. I cried all during this changing process. Back upstairs at the dinner table I sat blubbering for a while before I could settle down to eat.

"Stan Henderson's mother called," Mom said.

"What did she say?" I asked, dreading to hear the answer.

"She said you kicked poor little Stan several times and they had to take him to the hospital." Mom was nearly six-feet tall and she weighed nearly three hundred pounds. She had dark hair, but her complexion was as pale as a redhead's, and when she got upset her face turned beet red, that's the color it was when she told me about Stan.

"Christ on a crutch . . . so, keep going," Dad said, fixing a set of periwinkle-blue eyes, on Mom. Apparently he hadn't heard the entire story.

"Well, he has contusions on his back and ribs, and a broken bone in his wrist." She shook her head in disbelief. "What would possess you to do such a thing? It was mean . . . awful."

I shrugged.

"Now we have to pay his medical expenses," Dad said, "right at the time I was planning on investing in a new sawmill, that Greenlee Heavy-Duty 6-knife Double Surfacer," he said, seeming to take pride in giving us the tedious nomenclature of the sawmill of his dreams. "Now I'm going to have to wait to upgrade my sawmill business."

I didn't know a Greenlee sawmill from a lymph node, but I knew Dad was enraged about the matter and to not provoke him further.

"What would possess you to kick little Stan like that?" Mom asked.

It didn't seem advisable to tell her that Stan had merely tagged me "it." I decided to give them a more expansive explanation. "He has annoyed me for years. He is always hanging around and wanting to be my pal. I can't get away from him."

"Pat, that's the silliest thing I've ever heard. You kicked him for those silly little reasons? He's such a nice little boy."

"Yeah, that's about the size of it," I said, thankful I hadn't given her the unvarnished truth.

Mom passed a steaming bowl of mashed potatoes around the table and the gravy boat. "Pat, when he goes back to school I have a chore for you. He's in Mrs. Allred's class with you, right?"

"Right," I said, fearing what was to come.

"I want you to invite him over for cookies and milk, and then I want you to apologize to him in front of your father and me."

Two weeks later I approached Stan after I stood in front of the third-grade class and delivered a report on Arkansas. Anyway, after I completed the report and walked back to my seat, I leaned over and invited Stan to my house for cookies and milk. He still had a splint on his forearm supporting the broken wrist. The prospect of coming to my house for cookies and milk had him panting like a dog in heat, that's how eager he was to be my friend . . . go figure.

Back home that afternoon, the cookies and milk thing was a bummer. While Mom and Dad sat nearby, I apologized to Stan for kicking the shit out of him and I promised to be his friend. Mom had prepped me ahead of time on what to say. After pouring my heart out in a manner that seemed sincere, but was disingenuous as all hell, Mom cried, Dad smirked, Stan cried, and I came within a hair's breadth of barfing from the pure shock of being forced into participating in the charade.

Two days later, a classmate, Ronnie Mahoney—real name Ronald Theodore Mahoney, who lived across the street and was an electronics whiz kid gonzo about taking radios and telephones apart to see how they worked—and I staked Stan out in the horse pasture behind Mahoney's house. Ronnie and I looked for an anthill to put him on, but none was available. But to make it somewhat more like Indian torture, we did find some rawhide in Dad's tack

4

shed that we wet so that when the sun got at it, it would cut into his wrists and ankles. We got him stretched out in a nicely arranged spread-eagle and then we stripped off his shirt and left him to bake in the noontime sun.

It started out being a game—making believe we were renegade Indians—but it turned out being more serious, because we went off riding our bikes and forgot about him. By the time we remembered and got back to him he had a third-degree sunburn and the rawhide had dried and cut cruelly into his ankles and wrists.

When we cut him loose with an old hunting knife he was sobbing piteously, but he suddenly transformed from a pitiable, sobbing little boy into a raving lunatic. He grabbed a hatchet leaning against a nearby shed and chased me several city blocks until, thank the Lord, he gave up because he developed a stitch in his side. During the chase he swung the hatchet at me and tried with all his might to chop a divot from me. He actually got so close with one swing that he cut a slit in my new Levis. I didn't know he had it in him, he seemed like such a studious, harmless little shit.

Later that afternoon Dad came home from work. I was playing with my Lionel train set at the time. The tracks were laid out on a sheet of plywood and I was running the engine with seven cars around and around the track. I heard Mom and Dad talking quietly in the kitchen.

It never dawned on me why they were being so quiet until I realized Mom had just informed Dad that I'd taken part in staking out Stan to bake in the noontime sun. Dad walked into my bedroom where I was playing with the train set. He walked up smiling winsomely and punched me in the face. I went sprawling across the tracks on my back and derailed the train set. Then he simply walked out of the room and went in and sat down to dinner. The next day my eye, where the fist struck, was swollen shut. It was a good thing it was summer vacation because I didn't have to go to school and have everybody gawking at it. It took the eye about a month to fully heal.

"Christ on a crutch," Dad said, when I took a seat at the dinner table. "Now I have another hospital bill to pay. If you continue with this bullshit I'll never put together enough money to upgrade to the Greenlee Sawmill."

"Stan had to go to the hospital for a little ol' sunburn?" I asked, incredulous.

"It wasn't a little ol' sunburn," Dad said, his periwinkle-blue eyes transfixing me with hatred. "He had a third-degree sunburn. By the time they got him to the hospital he was in shock and suffering from dehydration. His parents said he's in terrible pain."

"Sorry, I didn't mean—"

"Shut up, you rotten little bastard," Dad snapped

Mother cried out, "He's just a little boy."

"Well, I think he has a screw loose," Dad said.

They sat there talking about me like I wasn't there, it was the strangest thing.

"Maybe we should take him to see the Bishop, get him some spiritual counseling," Mom suggested. "I want him to be happy. After all, he's my little boy and I love him dearly."

"No, Brenda, just no," Dad said.

"But maybe he just needs a little guidance."

"The only guidance he's going to get is at the end of my fist."

Mom noticed my eye that was beginning to swell shut. "Good heavens, you didn't punch him in the eye, did you, Morlin?"

"Yeah, I did."

"You shouldn't do that, he's only a little boy."

"Don't propose to tell me what I should or should not do, Brenda, or you'll get a little of the same," Dad said.

Here's the thing about Dad, a man who has long since gone to his reward. He went to church every Sunday, carried his Bible and thumped hell out of it, and I think he really believed in the gospel and the teachings. But during the other six days of the week he seemed to fall short on practicing what the LDS Church taught. I know for certain that it didn't say anything in the Book of Mormon, Bible, Pearl of Great Price, or Doctrine and Covenants about using a fist on naughty children or willful wives. Yes, he used his fist on Mom a couple times.

Two weeks later, as my battered eye got looking better, I got baptized by immersion at the stake house over in Kamas, Utah. Baptism is the fourth article of faith in the Mormon religion and must be performed by a qualified member of the priesthood. They had a baptismal font there. A member of the holy priesthood dunked me under the water, but some of my hair stayed above the water, so he was required to dunk me a second time. According to LDS rule, the entire body has to be immersed or the baptism isn't complete. Baptism symbolizes the death, burial, and resurrection of Jesus Christ. Baptism originated with St. Philip the Apostle and John the Baptist. They were the first to be baptized in biblical times, in order that they could gain entry into heaven. Ostensibly, my baptism made me a new man and it erased all of my sins and transgressions up to that point and paved the way for me to gain entry into heaven.

After the Elder who baptized me finished, I turned and whispered a question in his ear. "If I happen to mess up again, can I get this done again?"

He laughed. "No, son, I'm afraid not. It's a one-time deal." He probably wouldn't have laughed if he knew what I was capable of—what I'd done to Stan Henderson.

Stan, incidentally, had just been baptized the week before. He had been proud of taking part in the sacred ceremony. In fact he had been boasting about it all week and talking about his clean slate. It was ridiculous. I have always thought that if Stan's brains were dynamite, he wouldn't have enough to blow off the top of his head.

Things went pretty smooth for a couple years until I reached the 5th grade at Kamas Elementary School. They bused us from Oakley to Kamas each school day—some 15 miles. I attended a classroom that had grades three through six at the Kamas Elementary School. During that two-year interim, I only had the razor strap taken to me twice and I received no fists in the face.

Things went swimmingly until the day Ronnie Mahoney and I went down into his basement and commenced shooting his BB gun through the crack in a broken window. We were expert shots with the BB gun and could hit anything up to about fifty yards. We took turns shooting hubcaps on

7

passing automobiles, dogs, and bicycle fenders, and then we got bold and shot old Zeke Snider in the ass just as he was climbing back into his Weber River Creamery milk delivery van after delivering bottled milk to the Mahoney household. Zeke hopped around rubbing his ass for a while and using some vulgar language. I suppose he figured out what happened because later that day he ratted us out to my dad. That night Dad and I met at the laundry chute and he gave me ten lashes with the razor strap.

Later that summer, being a slow learner, I got involved with the BB gun again. The crack in the window commanded a view of a horse pasture alongside our home that was across the street. Dad had an Arabian horse, which he used for breeding purposes and held the stallion in high esteem. Dad's Arabian was cropping away at some meadow grass and I placed a BB dead center on one of his prized testicles. I'd never seen anything like it. He whinnied, started bucking and then he streaked around and around the pasture. It was an amazing spectacle. He had his tail up and was racing like the wind.

Ronnie and I laughed until we were sick, then we settled down and got involved in the shortened version of Monopoly. After we finished the game we took up the BB gun and Ronnie put a BB right on the knob of the Arabian stallion's manhood, or in this case, I suppose I should refer to it as his horsehood—for some reason he'd decided to extend it. The thing was hanging down about two feet. After being shot with the BB the stallion went into the same gyrations as before, except this time it was more pronounced. I suppose there are a lot of exposed nerves there on that knob. It was a sight to behold, that ol' stallion racing around the pasture with his horsehood flopping about like crazy. The thing flopping around like that must have hurt like the devil.

Quite predictably, we laughed ourselves silly—until Dad burst into Ronnie's basement bedroom and used the razor strap on both of us. Apparently, he had been watching his prized stallion out the kitchen window and had put two and two together.

I never realized just how effeminate Ronnie was until I listened to his shrill shrieks when Dad put the strap to his ass. After Dad left, Ronnie and I ran around his bedroom rubbing our behinds and bawling and shrieking to beat the band. It was a shameful display. But like I said earlier, every place that razor strap made contact it felt like a blow torch had been at work.

Later that afternoon Dad, and Ronnie Mahoney's dad, had a fist fight on our front porch. Ronnie's dad had gone temporarily insane with rage—as well he should have: Dad had invaded his home without invitation and had beaten the crap out of his son with a razor strap. But the fight was short-lived because Dad knocked him down with a bone-crunching straight right and Mr. Mahoney—even though his judgment was clouded by unbridled rage— retreated like a whipped pup—and it was the smart thing to do because he was hugely outclassed.

The events of that day were gossiped about in Oakley, Utah, for years to come, and the participants in the sordid little affair became part of local folklore.

Two years later, I was baptized for the dead in the Salt Lake temple. Apparently, Joseph Smith, back in 1837, came up with the concept while reading about the practice in the Old Testament. It was a ritual practiced in Solomon's Temple. The first LDS baptismal font was erected in Nauvoo. The font itself was constructed of wood and sat on the back of twelve carved oxen, patterned after the most perfect six-month-old steer they could find in the region. Later when the saints were driven out of Nauvoo by their neighbors for practicing polygamy, they reassembled in the Salt Lake Valley and built a new baptismal font in the newly constructed temple. The temple itself was constructed out of quartz monzonite that was quarried from nearby Little Cottonwood Canyon. The new baptismal font was, likewise, placed on the back of twelve oxen and it was even more splendid than the one abandoned in Nauvoo, just before the saints were run out of there by an angry mob of Illinois and Missouri farmers. The Mormons were reviled because of polygamy and their religious beliefs.

In order to enter the highly consecrated Salt Lake temple, I had to get a temple recommend, which I could only attain because I'd been quite well behaved during that period.

Baptism for the dead was revived by Joseph Smith back in 1840, He read about it in the New Testament, Corinthians 15:25. It was practiced by early

Christians, although it was forbidden by the Orthodox Church in the 4th century as being aberrant. It is the practice whereby a living person is baptized by proxy for a dead one of the same gender, in order that the dead person can gain entry into heaven.

I enjoyed the experience there at the Salt Lake temple. I felt the spirit of the Lord when I entered those hallowed chambers. The baptismal font itself was a thing of beauty. When it was my turn to be baptized for the dead I stepped bravely into the font, looking for a new experience. The man performing the baptism called my name, and said: "Having been commissioned by Jesus Christ, I baptize you for and in behalf of—full name of deceased person, whose name has gone clean out of my head—who is dead, in the name of the Father, and of the Son, and of the Holy Ghost, Amen." Then, as the proxy, I was dunked briefly into the water. We repeated this solemn ceremony fifteen times. When it was over I felt rather righteous. I was proud that I'd been part and parcel, if you will, of helping fifteen lost souls gain entry into the Kingdom of God.

Two weeks later I coaxed Mary Ellen Epperson into a neighbor's barn and molested her. I talked her into playing "Doctor." It was so exciting I thought I was going to burst. I'd never seen a little girl's what's-it. But as usual, there was a downside to the adventure: I became ridden with guilt over what I'd done and, last but not least, Dad found out and took the razor strap to me. Mostly though, I was mortified that I'd been caught doing such a naughty thing.

Mary Ellen was apparently mortified as well, because she confessed her sins to her mother, which is how Dad found out. I suppose Mary Ellen felt guilty because it didn't take a whole lot of persuading to convince her to play our sordid little game. She probably felt like she should have held out longer, you know, made me beg a bit. Anyway, I got fifteen lashes for that fun time activity and I had some award-winning welts that lasted for nearly two weeks. It was at that time that I noticed I was getting some scarring from all the razor strap strikes I had received over the years. The back of my legs and my behind looked like a battlefield.

Dad finally got his new Greenlee Sawmill and he hired more lumbermen and expanded his business. The sawmill business must have started making a lot more money because we moved into a new home that was nearly twice as large as the old one. It was a Raised Ranch style and it nicely reflected the Garley's improved economic standing in the community. Need I say that I was happy the new home didn't have a laundry chute?

Shortly after we moved into the new home, Mom was appointed president of the Relief Society. She had been a long-time member of the worldwide sisterhood whose members were devoted to Jesus Christ, savior and exemplar. Dad got a new calling as well. He was appointed the new Bishop of the Oakley Ward. But not to be outdone, I rose in the world as well. I became a priest in the LDS church and I sat in front of the congregation every Sunday and blessed the sacrament just before the deacons walked along the aisles to pass it out. Not only that, I joined the Boy Scouts and attended meetings every Tuesday evening at the Oakley Ward. I earned over thirty merit badges and I eventually became an Eagle Scout. Indeed, things went swimmingly for a while and Dad's razor strap was used for the sole purpose of putting a nice edge on his straight-edge razor.

Just when I thought I'd outgrown the tendency to stray from the straight and narrow, I broke two covenants with the LDS Church. I started having sex, lots of it. When I finally stopped to take a break, it wasn't out of guilt; it was due to a rather severe case of scrotal fatigue, I'm not kidding.

Then I committed an even more serious sin. Ronnie Mahoney and I got shit-faced on straight grain alcohol that we mixed with Hawaiian Punch. I'd just gotten my driver's license the day before and Dad let me take out his fin car, a 1959 Chevrolet Impala, to put it to good use.

I flipped the Impala off the Francis Dugway and killed Ronnie. Francis is a smallish, nearby community.

The only reason I wasn't killed was because I was ejected with the car's first roll. The car continued on without me, rolling an unspecified number of times until it reached the bottom of the Dugway, and that ass over tea kettle tumble pretty much turned Ronnie into blood puddin'.

Six months later, when I got out of the LDS Hospital in Salt Lake, and after I got feeling better, Dad came into my bedroom one afternoon after he had gotten off work. "Christ on a crutch, you truly are an evil little sunuvabitch," he said. "Now that alcohol has passed over your lips you have been tainted and are no good for anything. And another thing: I believe you've been having sex out of wedlock. If this is true, words alone cannot describe the contempt I feel for you!" He shook his head in disbelief. "How do you think the Lord feels about you at this time?"

I shrugged, not daring to say anything for fear he wouldn't like it.

"If you imbibe in alcohol again while you are under this roof I'll throw you out on your miserable little ass, do you understand?"

"Yeah."

"Oh, one more thing, what are you going to do if you get some girl pregnant?"

I just shrugged again, not daring to say anything.

Then he gave me a working over with the razor strap. It was the worst beating I'd ever taken with the thing and it hurt me so bad that Mom debated on whether I should go back to the hospital. In the end, I just stayed in bed for another week until I healed. Mom kept the welts and broken skin rubbed down with Bag Balm while I convalesced.

He left the mudroom after beating me half to death, shaking his head in disgust and disbelief. I suspect that at that time he feared he had spawned the devil incarnate—and perhaps he had. I'm sorry to say I just couldn't help myself back then. My behavior seemed to be controlled by demons; it depressed me and filled me with self-loathing.

I continued attending church after the accident, but it was difficult because Ronnie's mother was always there looking at me with her moist doe-eyes. There was a second reason attending church was difficult. Dad and his counselors discussed whether it was advisable to excommunicate me and that made it tense. In the end they decided against it and started working particularly hard at rehabilitating me and saving my soul.

Life for the next few years just seemed to drain away, like sand dribbling through an hourglass. It was amazing how fast it slipped away. I graduated from Summit High School in Kamas, Utah, and then I matriculated at Brigham Young University in Provo, Utah. I declared a major in English literature. I decided I wanted to teach it on a high school level.

A lot of people couldn't believe, because they had a low opinion of me, that I had an interest in English literature. They thought I'd be better suited just getting a job at my dad's sawmill or as a grease monkey in a local automobile repair shop.

During my sophomore year I met a girl named Jodie Hiatt from Payson, Utah. Her parents owned a pharmacy. She was over six feet tall, blond, and sexy as hell. Two months later we married and bought a starter home in Kamas. It was a small ranch-style home with several outbuildings and a horse corral. I continued attending BYU. I commuted there five days a week and I was maintaining a 3.875 grade point average. Life was good, I loved my wife immeasurably and I'd gotten away from dad and that razor strap.

But more importantly I'd cleaned up my act. It appeared I'd changed for the better. For the first time in a long time, I was actually starting to like myself.

It was at that time that Stan Henderson ingratiated himself back into my life. He called up one day and asked me if I'd board an old pinto mare that he used for a saddle horse. I agreed to it reluctantly and put his horse in the corral with my dun pony. I agreed to board the animal for $100 per month. I would provide the water and hay, everything, and he'd write me a check, without fail, each month for the specified amount.

New Year's Eve was approaching and my new bride talked me into inviting Stan and his new wife, Frieda Winterton, who hailed from Wallsburg, Utah, to a New Years Eve party. I tried to explain to Jodie that I hated Stan's guts, but she wouldn't hear of it and insisted I invite him. She thought the little twerp was charming as all hell.

Stan and Frieda showed up that New Year's Eve and we all got shitfaced on cheap whiskey and Coca Cola. After I got knee-crawling drunk I worked myself into a snit because Stan was late with a payment for his horse's keep. I pulled a .357 magnum out of a holster hanging on the back of a dining room chair and headed to the horse corral.

Stan followed, yelling at me, wondering what I intended to do.

I took aim at his Pinto when we arrived at the corral.

"Holy shit, what are you doing?" Stan yelled.

"What'n hell's it look like, you mooching little bastard? You're late with your payment, so I'm gonna shoot your goddamn horse right between the blinkers."

Stan stepped between me and the horse. "Don't you *dare* shoot ol' Patty!"

"Okay," I said, "then how about I shoot you, instead?" I took aim and shot him in the chest with a 120 grain .357 magnum bullet. He just stood there for an instant with his mouth trying to form a word, then he crumbled to the ground. Just before he died he did finally manage to utter one word, "Why?"

Unfortunately, I didn't have an answer to that.

My dad ended up selling his sawmill to pay several high-priced attorneys to defend me in a murder trial. It paid off because they got me off on a technicality. I actually only spent two months in jail. I'd simply lied and said I hadn't known the gun was loaded. The bullet that was fired had been in the chamber for years and it was corroded, and that corroded artifact helped corroborate my contention that I didn't know the handgun was loaded. I told the court that I only intended to click the trigger and frighten the little twerp.

I argued, "How was I to know there was a bullet in the chamber, put there years earlier?"

But make no mistake, I knew the bullet was there and even though it was old, I knew there was a high probability that it would fire.

The trial was a scandal in the sanctimonious and tiny community of Oakley, Utah. My wife divorced me. My parents spent so much on high-priced lawyers that they were forced into bankruptcy and they spent their doddering years dead broke, and I became a pariah. So what the hell, I decided to bail and settle in Nauvoo, Illinois, go back to where the Church gained great strength, a place steeped in church history. I needed to learn the LDS teachings from the bottom up, this for my salvation. Plainly put, I am hoping for atonement because I have a morbid fear of going to hell. But of equal importance, I want to gain forgiveness for all the death and misery

I caused people during my early years. I want my victims to be blessed and made whole.

Now my life is simple. I make a modest living operating a cleaning service. I clean many of the historical homes and businesses that were originally constructed by the LDS pioneers here in Nauvoo. I clean the Zion's Mercantile, the Joseph Smith Mansion House, and the Red Brick Store, among others. I never miss a church meeting and I pay a full ten percent tithe. I love Nauvoo; it is idyllic and beautiful. I bear my testimony during every sacrament meeting and I am sincere in it. According to LDS doctrine—faith without works is not enough. So I'm trying with all my heart to talk the talk and walk the walk. Never a day goes by that I don't perform some kindness for a fellow citizen.

According to the LDS Church, there are three kingdoms of glory after death: celestial, terrestrial, and telestial. I figure I have a pretty good chance at reaching one of the top two tiers which offer fuller eternal rewards. If I were only to reach the bottom tier, the Telestial Kingdom, that would mean I'd have to linger there, proving my worth for a thousand years before God would take me into his embrace. Of course, if I failed to land a spot on any of the top three kingdoms of glory, I'd end up being a "son of perdition" and languish forever in what the LDS refer to as "the outer darkness."

Murder in and of itself, according to LDS doctrine, is not an unpardonable sin. "God has a way out for you. Come through the door." John 10:9. I suppose I won't know if I have truly "gone through the door" until Judgment Day. Right now, only God truly knows.

I find love in my heart where I once found hate, tolerance where I once found scorn. There simply is no way to fake it where God is concerned. God is all-knowing. Never a day goes by that I don't consider that this extra work in order to attain worthwhile eternal placement could have been avoided . . . if I just hadn't pulled that trigger and acted out those other despicable acts. My heart simply breaks with the knowledge of it, and as a result I am contrite and chastened. The truth about how one should conduct one's life had been there all along, promulgated by the very church I had been ignoring.

15

RESPONSIBILITIES

I met Chastity McWhorter at a Brigham Young University dance, in Provo, Utah, back in 1969. She had hair the color of burnished onyx, and features much like Demi Moore. Oh yeah, the girl was eye candy, just what an old lecher like myself needed to get the blood pumping. I didn't know it then, but Chastity had Cherokee blood. Her biological mother was from southern Florida, but she never knew anything about her father. She'd been raised by adoptive parents and both were straight Caucasian, and that was fine by her; she loved her adoptive parents, as we shall discern later.

My name is Justin Canty and I was a senior at BYU the night of that long ago meeting. Chastity was a freshman at the time and hadn't yet declared a major. Her college attendance ended about then . . . and this is due to the fact that she met me. We did a fast dance to the tune of "Do you Love Me?" and I liked the way she moved. It was as sexy as can be.

Then we did another fast dance to "Louie Louie" and I asked her for her telephone number. She lived in Deseret Towers, nestled up close to the Wasatch Front where the big white-washed "Y" is sprawled across the mountain.

The next day I called and asked her if she had a term paper on hand that covered the Lost Generation of American writers that expatriated to Paris in the '20s: Ernest Hemingway, John Dos Passos, Gertrude Stein, F. Scott Fitzgerald, et al., the *carpe diem* crowd.

She told me to go piss up a rope. No, she didn't actually say that, because she didn't use that sort of language, but her sentiments pointed me in that direction. I hung up and got to thinking about that flat-out refusal. I was

16

trying to understand it; certain other females had accommodated me by giving up their term papers, and whatever else I needed. Were my charms in decline? Thank God, some of the girls in my past had saved me when I'd been too lazy to produce my own work, but not Chastity. What was the deal with her?

Finally, I decided this was a girl with high moral fiber, and that maybe I should pursue her more fully. Back then I had the capacity to notice high moral fiber in others, but not the capacity to notice how woefully lacking it was in myself.

I called her the next day and asked her out on a date. She accepted, even though I had outed myself as a lessons cheat. Why? Well, I suppose, contrary to earlier fears, I still was quite charming. I was tall, rather good looking, and manly, and that opened doors for me during those long-ago days. Most women like to take men on as a project. They figure to change them for the better, to knock off the rough edges and find the gentleman hidden beneath. Maybe she looked at me as a project. I took her to a little pizzeria, the Italian Oven, located just off campus.

Three months later I made that lovely part-Cherokee girl mine. I married her, but I never did talk her into helping me cheat on homework.

We lived in a basement apartment just off campus. An elderly couple, the Chapman's, long-since deceased, rented us their basement apartment. The thing was about the size of a postage stamp. Chastity landed a job at a newly established and futuristic business located in nearby Orem, Utah. It went by the name of Cybernetics. They made minuscule computer chips, used in early computers, and in airplanes, telecommunications, rocketry, etc. If I remember correctly, China was one of their biggest clients. Chastity spent her working days looking through a microscope and welding together tiny wires. She got a stiff neck from her labors.

As for me, I was drawing money from Uncle Sam on the GI Bill. I'd just completed a tour of duty in Vietnam. Regardless, we barely generated enough money between the two of us to make ends meet, even if the rent on our little apartment was a mere forty dollars a month.

Almost a year to the day from when we got married I graduated from BYU with a BA in English literature. Chastity had helped put me through the last year of school.

But I didn't put my new degree to work and begin paying her back. No, of course not, that would have made too much sense. Instead, I chose a career selling Encyclopedias and Children's literature for a company named Classmate International. I hired on with them and took Chastity on the road. I was good at sales, so the company promoted me to sales manager. Before long I hired three salesmen to work for me, and I earned overrides on their sales, and, of course, I earned commissions on my own sales. We traveled in caravans and we roved all over the Intermountain West peddling our wares, living out of motels and eating in greasy restaurants.

But things got sour after a while because I got to drinking with the boys in the evenings and abandoning my new bride in cheap motels. She put up with it for a spell until we got to Bozeman, Montana. I returned to the Magnuson City Center Motor Inn that night in a drunken stupor, only to find that she had cleared out.

There was a note on the pillow that read: "I've had enough. I'm leaving you. I'm flying home to Orlando. You should be all right, you have your drunken friends to keep you company. I've taken all of the money because a flight to Florida is expensive. Don't come after me. Hatefully yours, Chastity."

I cried for a while that night; I actually blubbered like a little girl. I loved Chastity with all of my heart, I really did, but I also loved the bottle and running around with my friends.

I thought it over hard that sad night. I knew I had to give up the partying and my friends if I wanted to stay married. I rationalized that I'd been in a war for a long time and then I'd immediately begun several years of hard work for a college degree. I figured I needed a break, and that I needed to relax and have some fun. I reasoned there would be plenty of time later to snap out of it and go after her and put my nose to the proverbial grindstone.

Two months later we disbanded our little sales crew and went our separate ways. Life on the road had gone stale. I went back to my hometown, Spanish Fork, Utah, and teamed up with a fellow named Nathan Littledeer, a half-

Ute. We decided to go looking for work in Utah's oil patch over in the Uintah Basin. We borrowed my brother's 1967 Mustang California Special, a car faster than a speeding bullet—my old Volkswagen had gotten too tired to be of any further service; I guess I'd worn it out driving all over creation selling those encyclopedias.

Nathan and I went to Duchesne, Utah, and got hired on with a trucking firm that had a contract hauling water to quite a number of oil drilling sites in that region, projects mostly owned by Humble Oil and Drilling Company. That early 1970s central-Utah oil patch was going strong, which sent me and Nathan to Lambert Trucking and Excavating looking for work.

Lambert was running ten tanker trucks twenty-four hours a day, providing nearby oil wells with water. The oil rigs used thousands of gallons of water each day, mixing it with drilling mud to create a slurry that circulates through the drill bit to keep it cool and help remove the cuttings. Lambert needed drivers the day we popped in looking for work. Nathan had experience driving the big rigs, so Ed Terry, the Lambert foreman, hired him right off and then turned to me.

I didn't have experience so I had to improvise, which is just a nice way of saying I lied. An unknown author once said: "A lie is an abomination unto the lord, and an ever-present help in the time of trouble." Well, I had a time of trouble, I needed work.

I told Ed I'd driven a Freightliner for Mayflower, a furniture moving franchise located in Grand Forks, North Dakota. He never checked that reference, nor did he ask me if I had a chauffeur's license, which I didn't. He just hired me and assigned me a truck, an old Mack Truck with eighteen forward gears. It was a 1957 B613T model. I remember those numbers for some reason, but I never knew what they meant. I think Terry assigned me that old Mack just in case I had the propensity to tear up machinery; it would minimize the company's losses. And I can't fault him for that. The old beast had a Browning gearbox that split nine forward gears, doubling the number. Going through eighteen forward gears takes a lot of shifting and leaves plenty of room for error, as I was to discover later.

I signed the papers, walked out into the shop and climbed up into the cab of the old Mack B613T. The dash looked like what I perceive a 747 Airliner's instrument panel would look like. I couldn't even figure out how to start the thing, much less drive it. So I found a mechanic and talked him into taking a ride around the block with me to show me how to operate it. I also urged him to keep his mouth shut about my inability to drive the thing. He drove me around the block and showed me how to shift the gears. Sometimes it required double clutching, and at other times he could just shift it without using the clutch at all.

I never did master most of the intricacies of a Mack truck.

I showed up the next day, filled the Mack with diesel and headed to the Duchesne River for water. Lambert had two big pumps on the Duchesne River that pumped water from the river and into the tankers. Luckily, there was another driver there filling his tanker so I asked the guy to show me how to pump water into my tanker. He showed me and before long I'd topped off the huge tank and was headed out to supply water to the first drilling rig on the list Ed Terry had earlier that morning handed me.

The Mack handled much differently filled fully with 28,000 pounds of water. I was so scared that my legs were trembling and I about wet my pants. It was winter, November, and the roads were ice-packed and slick, and there were some really treacherous mountain roads to negotiate. There were rock cliffs to one side and sheer drop-offs to the other. And to add to my problems, I ground the gears nearly every time I shifted. In fact, sometimes I missed a gear and simply could not find another, so I'd have to stop and start from scratch. I'd been told to use the gearing, up or down to control the truck's speed and to stay off the brakes as much as possible.

"If you burn out your brakes, boy, you could die," that old mechanic, my recent truck-driving instructor, had said. He elaborated that I should most especially learn to use the engine compression to hold me back on steep, downhill parts.

It was hard for me to let loose and rely on the compression to control my speed on the hills, and it didn't seem like the Jake Brake was working all that well. I worked the brakes quite regularly—I was afraid of ending up at the bottom of one of those rock-strewn canyons. I didn't breathe until I finally reached Nomac Drilling's rig #11 and pumped its tank full of water.

A nasty, dissipated, vile-looking, ancient Okie, the drilling foreman, came out and helped me, and that was a good thing, because I didn't have a clue about where I was suppose to pump the water. I didn't know how to pump water out of the tanker, period.

"Smells like ya burnt shit outa them brakes, boy. I'd suggest you learn to use the gearin' on this ol' Mack and lay offa those brakes . . . that is, if you've gotta notion to stay healthy."

"Thanks," I said, as I drove away. I went back to the Duchesne River, filled my tank and then headed out to find the Natchitoches field and begin filling the tanks out there. I think it was Humble Oil, not Nomac that was drilling in that particular oil patch.

During that first week I got a little better as a truck driver, but I didn't get so skillful that I felt an urge to run out and join the Teamsters and pledge myself to a career in trucking. Looking back on it, I can't believe that I didn't get discovered for the fraud I was, but Ed and my fellow truckers just never paid much attention to me. So I just drove around in that Mack, for the entire week, grinding the shit out of those gears. When Saturday rolled around the foreman told me to drive the Mack into Roosevelt to have the Jake Brake lash adjusted at a shop over there.

I'd been complaining that the Jake Brake wasn't holding me back all that well when I was loaded with 28,000 pounds of water and rolling downhill on ice-packed roads. I was having to rely on the brakes overly much, and prayer. There is an old saying about trucking: "Trucking is noted for having long hours of boredom punctuated by moments of sheer terror." Well, trucking for me was just the reverse of that: It was long hours of sheer terror punctuated by moments of boredom.

I headed to Roosevelt and drove out onto the open highway. That too was a scary endeavor. The road was slick and there were curves and traffic to deal with. I kept worrying I was going to lose control and crush some innocent motorists driving around in their gnat-like cars. I let out a long-held breath when I finally reached Roosevelt. I sighed and edged onto their main street and approached one of their stoplights. I thought I'd be professional about it and shift to a lower gear and let the compression slow me down, rather than risk applying the brakes and end up skidding on the ice.

I downshifted and let the clutch out and the tanker went into a skid. Apparently, I'd dropped it into a gear that was too low and the hind wheels just locked up when I released the clutch. The huge tanker skidded along and before I knew it I was going sideways. I was only going about ten miles an hour, but it wouldn't stop. The back end swung around and whisked by a line of parked cars. I could see it all happening in the Mack's big side mirror. I came so close to those cars that I probably scraped microbes off them. Then I continued out into the intersection and finally got stopped dead center under the traffic light.

So there I was, right in the middle of the intersection sitting all skewampus, and I was blocking traffic coming from all four directions. And all the cars, of course, honked at me from all four intersections and several gave me the finger while I backed up and drove forward several times to get the big tanker going straight again. It's kind of unnerving to be the object of such meanness.

When I finally arrived at a place called the Diesel Doctor, my nerves were shot, so I dropped the truck off and headed to a bar to have a couple beers and unwind. After sipping on a beer for a minute I walked over and dropped a quarter in a payphone and called Chastity in Orlando. She answered on the third ring. "Hello."

"Hello, Chastity, this is Justin, how are—"

"Are you drunk?"

"No, what would make you ask that?"

"Oh, I don't know, just a guess."

"Well, I'm not."

"It's a good thing, because if you were I wouldn't even give you the thirty seconds I'm allotting you."

"That's just mean. I'm not drunk."

"What do you want?"

"Will you take me back?"

"No."

"Why not?"

"You know why."

"I don't drink all that much . . . I just have a few beers sometimes, to unwind."

"What a laugh."

"Do you love me?"

"No."

"Yeah, you do . . . You know that you do."

"Justin, you have hurt me—hurt me."

"I know, but I can make it up to you, I—"

Click! The phone went dead. The silence was like a dagger to the heart. I was beginning to think maybe she really didn't love me anymore, that my drinking had killed any love she'd had for me. It was a scary thought, because I really did love her.

The operator came on the line and told me I owed another dollar, and to please make the deposit. I dropped four quarters in the slot, worked the lever up and down and dropped in another quarter. I dialed Lambert over in Duchesne.

Ed Terry answered. "Lambert Trucking and Excavating, can I help ya?"

"Hello, yeah, this is Justin, Justin Canty."

"Justin. What's up, kid? Did you make 'er into Roosevelt?"

"Yeah, but here's the thing: I'm quitting. Please have my check ready so that I can pick it up tomorrow."

"I'm a sad, sorry sunuvabich! Why're you quittin'?"

"Because you've got me in an unsafe truck. It's the worst I've ever driven."

"Worst you've ever driven? Who are you kiddin'? It's the only one you've ever driven. Do you think we didn't know? We let you get away with that bullshit story about drivin' for Mayflower, because we didn't have the time to train you. We have decided to let a few of you young liars slip through, without training. What the hell, we put you in the ol' Mack to see if you could pick it up by on-the-job-training. But it appears you don't have what it takes to be a trucker. You're too lazy and chickenshit."

23

"I'm not lazy, and I am sure as hell no chickenshit: I should kick your old—"

"Ah, save it. Just bring the Mack back and we'll cut ya a check."

"That's the thing. I'm not going to drive the Mack back, it's not safe."

"Bullshit, if ya think you're leavin' us in a lurch? Well, you've go another thing—"

I hung up. Here's the thing, I was too chickenshit to drive the Mack back to Duchesne. The trip into Roosevelt had scared me silly.

That night I talked Nathan into quitting Lambert. It didn't take much to persuade him, Nathan never had been too fond of working. We went into Lambert in the Mustang the next morning and picked up our paychecks. It was payday, so we didn't have any trouble getting our pay. Ed Terry came out of his office and walked us to our car. He wanted to make sure we were gone, for good, and that we didn't steal anything on the way out. Apparently they had had problems with that sort of thing.

"You guys have really put us in a bind this morning," Terry said, as he walked along with us.

"Tough shit," Nathan said.

"Ah, good riddance," Ed said.

"Ed," I said, "you need a bath. If you stood next to a decaying carp, there wouldn't be a fly on it."

"Why, I'll—" We peeled out before Ed got a chance to finish his threat.

We drove to Roosevelt that morning and began searching for work at the various drill sites. We thought we'd give rough-necking a try. Roughnecks are the coarse, profane, semi-skilled laborers who feed the pipe into the drilling hole. It's a dirty, nasty job, and exceedingly dangerous. As it turned out, it was easy getting work in the Central Utah oil patch there in the early '70s. Almost every drill site was short-handed. The third drill site we visited hired us on the spot; they needed roughnecks, two guys had just quit. We reported for work that night at midnight. The crew there on that drill rig called us worms: new guys that don't know anything.

Our employment was with La Point Oil, northeast of Roosevelt. The wells were being drilled by Creston Resources, Ltd. Many of the crew members at drilling rig #37 were from Texas and Oklahoma. They were men who moved from oil patch to oil patch. Most of them had worked all over the United States and at various locations overseas.

It didn't take long to figure out how many ways a roughneck could get badly injured, or killed. In fact, on that first night, the foreman gave me a job that could have easily gotten me killed. He gave me a huge pipe wrench and told me to climb the crow's nest and tighten four huge bolts that must have been four inches in diameter. The top of the crow's nest was at least a hundred feet up in the chilly night sky. It was a cold winter night and before I reached the halfway point I was shaking so badly I could hardly hold onto the ladder. I knew that if I fell it would be certain death, that I might even land square on the five-hundred-pound tongs used to add sections of pipe as the bore hole sunk deeper into the earth.

By the time I got up there I was a nervous wreck and my teeth were chattering. I took a few minutes to catch my breath, and then I managed to tighten the bolts. The wrench was incredibly heavy and the bolts were resistant and stubborn. It took a lot of power and leverage to so much as budge them, which was hard to do because I was concentrating on holding on to the ladder. When I started back down I noticed a steel cable that descended away in an arc and was fastened to the ground in an open field about fifty yards away. At the top of the cable was a device looking something like a bicycle. It was mounted to the cable. It had a little t-bar seat and foot pegs.

When I finally got back on the ground, I vowed to never climb that crow's nest again. I suspected those huge nuts hadn't really needed tightening at all, that the foreman had just sent me up there testing my mettle, and because I was a worm.

"Did you torque those bolts down?" the foreman asked as a faint little smile flashed momentarily across his face. "Those bolts hold the whole top of the crow's nest in place."

"Yeah, but who are you kiddin'? Those bolts were already so tight they'd hardly budge."

"They have to be really tight," the foreman said.

"I'm scared of heights."

I thought he was going to bust a gut laughing. "Scared of heights," he said, cackling like a hen.

"I'm serious, if you ask me to go up there again I'll quit so fast it will make your head spin."

"Around here, you do what you're told or get sent packing."

"Oh, well," I said, reconsidering. "What is that cable up there with the bicycle-like thing fastened to it? The one that stretches out to that field." I pointed to where the cable was anchored to the ground.

"That's called the Geronimo. Sorry, I forgot to tell you about it. If this drill site were to catch fire and blow while you were up there, you'd have needed to climb on that contraption, release the brake and scream Geronimo. Then, of course, you'd put the brake back on before you hit the ground."

"Jesus! Does that brake really slow you down before you hit the ground?"

"Very seldom. Riding the thing is usually fatal," he said, again cackling like a hen.

Nathan and I worked the oil patch about a week, only to discover that the work was too hard, too cold, and too dangerous. And the oil people working there were intolerable. They were hard-bitten, hard drinking, hard-assed sons-a-bitches. An oversized goon from Norman, Oklahoma, lit an oil-soaked rag on fire that was hanging from my back pocket. It singed my ass good before several roughnecks beat it out with their bare hands.

One night, during our stay there in Roosevelt, Nathan took me to meet his mother. His mother lit into him the moment we entered her double-wide trailer home. Apparently, she had a lot of issues concerning her son. Nathan had been in and out of jail for most of his adult life. He'd stolen cars, molested young women, robbed a service station, and he had written bad checks at one time or another.

At the time I didn't know about Nathan's past. I thought he was a pretty decent fellow—wild, yeah; drunken, yeah; loud-mouthed, yeah—but I hadn't known he was a felon. No wonder his mother was on his case. She was Caucasian and quite attractive for a middle-aged lady, but as I was to find out later, she was also mentally unstable. Nathan's Indian blood must have come from his father, who had died of emphysema a few years earlier. She hollered at him for ten solid minutes, airing old grievances.

It was embarrassing for me, standing their listening to it. She brought up things he'd done ten years earlier and excoriated him for them. Towards the end of our visit she told us to stay away from those Ute Indian women that lived in the area and then she told us to get out. I was treated as badly as her son, simply through association. It really wasn't fair. Finally, she insisted we leave, but we kept hanging around, hoping she'd feed us. A home-cooked meal seemed mighty appealing. She said that "Gunsmoke" was coming on TV and that she didn't want to miss it. "Remember about those Ute girls, they'll give you disease," she reminded us as we left.

Two nights later, we were edging the Mustang away from the curb after getting cheeseburgers from a Dairy Queen when Nathan suddenly got all chirpy. Apparently he'd run into an old friend in the restaurant's restroom and the guy had given him an invitation.

"Why are you so happy?" I asked.

"I ran into an old friend of mine in the liquor store," he said, still bubbling with glee. "There's going to be a party at his house tonight. He invited us. It should be a blast. Could you use a *mamaci* tonight? Who knows, you just might get our ashes hauled."

"What'n hell's a '*mamaci*'? I asked

"That's Ute for 'woman.'"

"I don't want my ashes hauled, and remember what your mama said about Ute women?"

"Who gives a shit?"

I ignored that and went off in another direction. "What's the guy's name?"

"Sammy Goldenbeaver."

"He's an Indian? A Ute?"

"Yeah. I went to school with him. He's a good head."

"That don't mean shit to a tree. I'm not going to a party thrown by Ute Indians. They would take my scalp."

"None of 'em would bother you because you'd be with me."

"No."

"The beer will be free."

"No."

"The party will be over in Randlett. I repeat, the beer will be free. The Ute's are going to have tons of suds, they always do." A muscle in his cheek was jumping.

"No. You're half Indian, you look like an Indian. I, on the other hand am white, I look white. It would be suicide for me to go to a party jam-packed with Ute Indians."

"What're you, a chickenshit?"

"No, just practical. As you should know, there's bad blood between whites and Indians . . . and those Ute's will all be shitfaced."

"There will be girls. Ute girls."

"Remember what your mother said about Ute girls, that they'll give us diseases."

"Come on."

"Ha! Are you beggin'?" I asked.

"Yeah, this party will be a blast. Come on, we'll only stay about an hour."

"No."

"Come on, don't be such a little pussy."

"Isn't Randlett all government housing, put in there for the Utes?"

"Yeah. So?"

"So, probably everybody that lives in Randlett is Ute."

"So?"

After a long back and forth, I finally caved in. "Okay! All right! I'll go to the Ute shindig for an hour, one hour, but I think I'm making a mistake."

Later that afternoon we lit off the Mustang and headed to Randlett to the Ute beer party. Before we found the party I pulled into a Rexall Drugstore and used a payphone. I decided I wanted to talk to Chastity. She answered after about the tenth ring; maybe she sensed it was me. "Hello, this is the McWhorter residence."

"Hi, Chastity this is—"

There was a huge click that came like a punctuation mark indicating it was over, our marriage was over . . . or so it seemed. It scared the hell out of me. I considered that perhaps I'd stayed away too long. I wondered what life would be like without my sweet Chastity. I really did love her, but I loved the bottle as well. I decided I needed to get away from Nathan, sober up, and go after her. But I was committed to go to that Ute party. I decided that if I survived the party I'd head for Florida tomorrow.

This great time I thought I'd have, drinking and being irresponsible hadn't really been such a great time. It had been a very bad idea. I needed to dry out and start thinking straight. Nathan and I'd been drunk for a solid month while working central Utah's oil patch. A reality check told me that I'd been soused longer than a month; actually, I'd been soused ever since I'd graduated from BYU, about five months before. While I'd been at that devout school of faith, an offshoot of the LDS church, I'd watched my P's & Q's. But after I got away from its religious, humbling influence I'd fallen apart, become a drunk.

I was truly ashamed of myself.

The beer party at a Ute's home was well underway when we got there. They had a coffee table stacked with cases of beer and they had a stereo blasting out '70's dance music. "A Horse with No Name" was blaring through the speakers, coming near to breaking my ear drums. Those Indian people were having a great time, dancing, laughing, talking, and every last one of them was slobbering drunk.

Nathan immediately went after the prettiest Ute Indian girl in the place and had her in the middle of living room, dancing to a Jimi Hendrix guitar solo that just started up. I remember being a little sad listening to Hendrix, he'd died a couple months earlier attending a party in London, and I was wondering if I was going to die attending this party in Randlett.

But I was really drunk, as usual, and I didn't dwell on it for too long. Instead I sidled over and asked an Indian girl to dance. She turned me down flat. I guess she didn't like the looks of me. Perhaps she only got off on the darker Indian types. Or maybe she was protecting me from the men in that room. It didn't really matter, a little later they came at me anyway, in a murderous mob.

Shortly after asking the Indian maiden to dance I wandered over to make buddies with some of the men, but they wouldn't have any of it. Maybe they were remembering the Little Big Horn, or Wounded Knee, but, more than likely, it was simply because they didn't like the looks of my white face.

I was beginning to feel left out when a young Indian boy sidled over to me as if he wanted to be pals. *Good*, I thought, *at least one of them doesn't despise me.* But I quickly changed my mind when an older Indian pushed the young one standing next to me and sent me reeling across the floor. A few minutes later it happened again, so I knew at that point that their actions were done on purpose. The third time this happened I exploded in a blind rage. I stiff-armed one of the Indians in the face and the other in the chest. I'm a big guy and I sent them flying across the room. The older one, the shover, slid into the television and knocked it over, and the one who'd been shoved into me took the legs out from under the coffee table and the beer came crashing down on him. That brought the whole Ute Nation down on me, or so it seemed.

About six or seven of them came at me and started throwing fists. I got shoved into a corner, which was good because they couldn't get in behind me. I got struck in the face a number of times. Thank heavens none of them had much of a punch. The blows hurt, yeah, but they weren't stunning, crushing blows that would've incapacitated me. I got lined out on two of them and put them both down with a nicely placed left jab and a right hook. And that was a good thing because that backed the war hoops up some, made them pause.

After putting two of them down, they had an idea of what a real punch is like and it apparently frightened them, because they stopped punching at me. So, we had ourselves a standoff, we stood cursing each other and trading threats, you know, posturing, long enough for me to get really scared. I figured when the next wave of blows came that there'd be so many of them, you know, a fist storm, that they'd probably kill me.

About that time, though, before round two got started, the owner of the house shot off a twenty-two revolver into his ceiling. "Get back you drunken assholes," he screamed. "You're destroyin' my home! I'm gonna take this paleface out on the porch and shoot his sorry ass . . . because I don't want his blood in my house."

He lowered the revolver and aimed it at my face. I was looking down the dark, deadly bore, expecting any second to be shot in the face. "Come on, now, don't shoot," I said, "there are a house full of witnesses, you'll go to prison, you'll end up on death row."

"Ugh, me want 'um firewater," he said, parodying the stereotypical Hollywood Indian. Everyone laughed hysterically, like the guy was Red Skeleton, or the like. Little did they care that I was about to get my face shot off. One of the merrymakers handed him a bottle of scotch and he tipped it up and took a slug, perhaps fortifying himself for what was to come. "Shut up and get your ass out on the porch," he continued, making his voice come across grave and serious. "Why'd you come here anyway? You loco in the head?"

The crowd cleared back and I sidled along with my back to the wall, all the time looking down that deadly bore. When I reached the door, not taking my eyes off that gun, I reached behind me, found the door knob, opened the door, and stepped out onto the porch. Then I went skidding on a patch of ice and fell off the porch onto the sidewalk. It shook me up a little and I skinned my knee and a hand, but I wasn't badly hurt.

The homeowner laughed, then shut the door behind him, bounded down the steps and stuck the revolver in my face. *This is it*, I thought. *This is how it ends. I won't even get a chance to go after sweet Chastity.* "Run, you bastard, run," the homeowner whispered, making me his co-conspirator. "That bunch of drunken heathens in there wants your ass."

I ran. When I got to the Mustang, Nathan was in there with the pretty Indian girl, his dance partner. I fired up the Mustang and gunned it to get out of the mouth of the drive. Then I looked in the rearview mirror and saw all those pissed-off Indians running toward the car. Now I know how Custer must have felt.

It was winter and the drive was snow packed, and there was a slight rise coming up out of the drive to the road. The Mustang had cheater slicks, racing tires, and all we did was spin and inch ahead, the Utes still coming. But just before they reached us I hit dry pavement on the roadway and we were off, fishtailing, with the glass packs bellowing and the tires squealing like they were being tortured.

"You're a chickenshit, Nathan," I shouted, "why didn't you jump in and help me back there? The two of us could have taken 'em!"

"Because, I was gettin' lined out with this *mamaci*." He smiled at the girl. "'Sides, it wasn't my fight."

"Remember what you said, that I'd be perfectly safe at an Indian party?"

"Hell, I didn't know you were going to knock a couple of 'em down like that. What did you expect?"

"Help."

"Well, you didn't get help, did you?" he said, as a muscle just below his left eye jumped. I could see it in the moonlight. He was riding shotgun with the girl between us and he had his head craned around looking at me. I caught the twitch in the moonlight. "Let's go to the motel," he said.

"I'm pulling out of here tomorrow. I'll hitchhike to Florida if I have to, to see if Chastity will take me back. I've had enough of all this bullshit. I've had enough of you."

"Good riddance."

"You won't have any wheels. I'm returning this Mustang to my brother, who lives in Goshen."

"Doesn't matter, I'm going to take this girl," he pointed to the Indian girl, "and we'll get on over to Grand Junction, Colorado, and boost a car. Then me and this girl are gonna hit the road, you know, see the United States. Aren't we, sweetheart? Hell, we're gonna screw in every state in the union, set some kinda record." He looked to the girl for confirmation and got a timid little nod.

"Sure you are. What about money? How will you finance this trip?" I asked.

"A couple heists will take care of that. Shit, this gal and I are gonna be a modern-day Bonnie and Clyde." He stopped and thought things over for a minute. "Hey, you can leave tonight, for all I care. I'm sick of ya." I supposed it would serve no purpose to remind him that Bonnie and Clyde, in the end, had died in a lead storm

"No, I paid half for the room and I'm gonna get a good night's rest."

"Whatever suits you just tickles me plumb to death," he said.

"What's your name?" I asked the girl.

"I am Ute," the girl said, in this faint, squeaky little voice.

"No, I didn't ask for the name of your tribe. I asked for your name."

"I am Ute. Lots of Indian girls have the name 'Ute,' it means hill people. I'm a person from the hills. I am Ute the Ute."

"Right," I said.

"Why'd you shove those guys?" she squeaked.

"They were bumping into me, on purpose. I couldn't let 'em get away with it."

"A *Tangwaci* at that party had a knife. You're lucky he didn't stick it in your gizzard."

"*Tangwaci*? What the hell's that?" I asked.

"In the language of the Ute, that is 'man,'" Ute the Ute said.

"I can't speak Ute, so can't we just speak English here?" I asked, being as polite as I could; I'd alienated enough people for one day.

"Yeah, white man, yeah. We can speak English. I have good English," she squeaked.

"Good, anyway, Ute the Ute," I said, chuckling a little, "I know I'm lucky that I didn't get cut, shot, or bludgeoned. If it hadn't been for the guy that owned that house . . ." We rode in silence the rest of the way.

The room had twin queen-sized beds. I slept in one and Nathan and Ute the Ute in the other. About an hour after we turned in I heard some stirring from the adjoining bed. I was on my side facing them when I heard gasping and grunting, so I opened my eyes and finally managed to get them focused on two dark forms on the other bed. Apparently Nathan was getting started on his pledge to do it in every state in the union; and, hooray, he could cross Utah off the list. I could see Nathan's rear-end under the covers, sliding back and forth as he plunged in and out of her. I could hear her stifled gasps. They were on their sides, with her back to him. They were doing it easy and quiet, hoping I wouldn't know what was going on. I suppose they thought if he got on top, missionary style, that it would be too obvious. Watching them secretly like that made me feel like a voyeur, and it managed to get me worked up . . . a cold shower might have helped. I missed my little Chastity.

Somebody knocked on the door. I got up and slipped on my trousers and went to answer it.

"Damn it, let us get some clothes on," Nathan said.

But I was annoyed with Nathan so I marched over and opened the door and there stood Nathan's mother. She saw her son in bed with Ute the Ute and she went ape-shit. She streaked across the room and went for Ute's face with her long fingernails. Nathan hopped out of bed, naked, and held his mother back. In retaliation she pulled her nails across his back and raked him to the bone. He screamed. He had four bloody streaks that ranged across where his right kidney was located.

His mother was cursing Ute the Ute and screaming at the top of her lungs, Ute the Ute was screaming, Nathan was screaming, and I was laughing like a halfwit. It was like a loony bin.

Mama was psychotic, and she'd been drinking. I could smell the whiskey fumes.

Nathan shoved her to the door and out on the sidewalk. "Get out of here, you crazy ol' bitch," he screamed as he slammed the door.

I couldn't help it, I kept laughing. The sight of Nathan wrestling his mother to the door with his wobblies flopping about was a sight I'll never forget. But my laughter was short-lived because a huge rock come sailing through a front window pane in a shower of glass splinters, then another pane was taken out.

Nathan snatched the door open to prevent more damage. It was a cold night and the room instantly cooled down. As soon as mama entered the room she went on a beeline for Ute the Ute. Ute had coal black hair that reached all the way to her shoulders and mama buried her fingers in it and dragged her from the bed. It had to have hurt like the devil. Ute the Ute was naked too and that sight is also burned indelibly in my mind's eye. Her boobs were flopping around, as was her butt cheeks and belly fat. She was a little on the chunky side and that made things a little floppy.

I saw her nether end from several angles that can only be described as visual blight. The sight of it almost made me swear off sex, almost.

The screaming started anew. Ute had her mouth wide open and she was screaming bloody murder, Nathan's mother was screaming, Nathan was screaming, and, admittedly, I too had given in to it and was screaming at the top of my lungs. The four of us were in a full-blown psychotic state.

"You slut," Mama screamed. "I am going to kill you for screwin' my son . . . you slut," she repeated in a high-pitched shrill, then, catching her breath and picking it up louder than ever, "I imagine you're pullin' the train for both of these pigs, aren't you, a slut like you?"

I didn't even know the woman and she was calling me a pig and sexual deviant. It was evident that Mama hated Ute Indians to the point of derangement. Perhaps it was because she'd been married to a Ute who turned out being a bum. But I guess I'll never really know what made mama go nuts. Perhaps it was just the whiskey.

Nathan and I were astonished at the speed with which his mother crossed the room and attacked Ute. After she got her hands buried in the girl's hair, we stepped in to help. Keep in mind, that both Ute and Nathan are naked. Nathan picked his mother up off the ground and tried to yank her away from Ute, but it didn't work, it only caused Ute a great deal of pain, because she got dragged into the bathroom by her hair.

I took hold of Mama's hands and tried to pry them loose from Ute's hair. But no matter how hard I tried, I couldn't break the grip. Ute's hair was falling out in clumps. I'm large and strong, but I couldn't break Mama's grip. It was unbelievable. As mentioned earlier, the four of us tumbled into the bathroom, sort of like a ball of writhing snakes, and parts of the motel room got broken in our wake: the foot board on the bed, a coffee table located between the beds, the wall, the bathroom mirror, and a medicine cabinet. And we were all bleeding from little cuts.

"Let loose of her, Ma, or I am going to knock your block off," Nathan yelled, balling up his fist and holding it up to her face.

"Go ahead, hit your mother," Mama said, jutting out her chin, "and I'll have you thrown in jail for assault."

"Assault, ha, assault," Nathan grunted. "What would you call what you're doing to Ute?"

"You haven't seen anything yet, I'm gonna kill the slut," Mama shrieked.

Ute let out a piercing scream.

Everybody was grunting, whining, cussing, and the air was redolent with sweating bodies, and the unmistakable odor of recent sex. It was a nightmarish experience, surreal. I was just getting ready to knock Mama unconscious, put a fist up to the side of her head when the unexpected occurred: Mama suddenly let loose of Ute's hair, stood there a moment all prissy like and picked strands of cold black hair from between her fingers, and dropped it on the floor.

We watched this spectacle in complete silence. Mama was regal like in manner and it was obvious that she was repulsed by Ute the Ute's hair entwined in her fingers. After cleaning herself up nicely, she lifted her head all dignified-like and marched to the door. But before she passed through the door, she turned and spoke to Nathan. "Put some clothes on. You look ridiculous with that little wiener of yours flopping around. It's so tiny, like your worthless father's."

"You're a crazy old bitch," he shouted.

"Maybe so, but if you ever need to stop by the trailer to borrow money or for other favors, you'd best be shed of this slut."

"Ma, someday I'm gonna kill you . . . you're a drunken, crazy old battle-axe."

"Yeah, right, I figured you didn't have the guts for it . . . you're just like your ol' man." She stepped away and we heard her vomiting outside the motel room. The broken window panes conducted the sound rather handily. Then we heard her start her car and leave.

"Jesus," Nathan said, sighing, "Jesus."

While Nathan cussed, Ute pulled her clothes on and sobbed as if her heart were broken; perhaps it was.

I just stood there and leaned against the wall until my heart rate went back down. I'd come very close to coldcocking Mama. I might have killed her because I can hit like a mule. But you know, to this day I can't figure out why I didn't have the strength to pull Mama's fingers out of Ute the Ute's hair. I suppose Mama's strength had been quadrupled by rage, something like that. I glanced at Nathan; he was pulling on his underwear. I was looking forward to be shed of Nathan, the guy was a waste of good skin.

The next day I returned the Mustang to my brother in Goshen, some 125 miles east, and I stepped out onto the highway and stuck up my thumb. I couldn't ride a bus because I was flat broke. I had a raging headache from too much alcohol from the night before but what the heck, I was going to hitchhike to Orlando, Florida and try to get Chastity back. I had zip money to make the trip, zip. Try that sometime. The remainder of the paycheck had gone to paying off the damage to the motel room.

I was full of self-loathing that morning that had taken over my soul. I knew I had to put my life back in order or I'd soon be dead. I'd had a drink every day for nearly five months and I imagine my poor old liver had taken somewhat of a beating.

I caught a ride with a young couple on their way to Tucumcari, New Mexico, to be with the woman's mother, who was dying of lung disease. They lived in Salt Lake and they were both medical doctors and devout members of the LDS church. They talked about the mother in medical terms and the woman cried from time to time. I never did get their names. I was glad to get out of the car when they let me out at Montezuma Creek, Utah, located near the Four Corners region, a place where Utah, Colorado, Arizona, and New Mexico come together.

The couple was gloomy and gloomy wasn't what I needed at the time. I had my own gloom to contend with. I found a payphone at a gas station and called Chastity. Her father answered and when he recognized who it was he hung up, which made me mad. Then I got to thinking about it and I decided if our roles had been reversed I would've been equally as rude. Regardless, I was going after my little Chastity. I needed her back, I needed her desperately, she completed me.

When I got to Fort Smith, Arkansas, I called Chastity again. This time she answered the phone. "Hi," I said, "Chastity, I love you, listen, I—" The phone went dead.

When I reached Biloxi, Mississippi, I was five days into the hitchhiking expedition and I was almighty hungry. When people picked me up I'd hinted around that I was hungry and several had bought me meals in fast food restaurants, but it never seemed to be enough.

I also hinted around in the afternoons that I didn't have a place to stay. As a result of this shameless begging, a guy in Lubbock, Texas, had taken me home with him and let me sleep in an extra bedroom. In Macon, Georgia I spent the night in a homeless shelter. I spent one night in a sleeping bag a guy threw me before he disappeared into a warm motel room. These many years later I don't remember where I spent each and every night, but I managed somehow to always get in out of the cold.

I finally made it to the Florida panhandle and ran into a bit of luck. A trucker picked me up in Tallahassee, Florida. He was a black fellow and he was an owner/operator of a tractor and trailer. He was hauling a load of furniture for snowbirds from New York City to Orlando. That was perfect. I could ride with him all the way in. I wouldn't have to stick my thumb up again. But it got even better.

"Tell you what," he said. "I imagine you're broke and if you hope to get back with your honey, you'd best have some cash money, some walkin' 'round money." Then he went silent about it for a while. I watched him slide through the gears without a hitch, wondering how he did it. I decided that I hadn't been able to shift that old Mack because the transmission had been messed up, that the fault hadn't been mine. Finally, the black fellow continued his train of thought. "I s'pose you need money when you go after your honey?"

"Yeah, that would help."

"You'd better take'r to dinner or do somethin' nice, 'cause it sounds to me like you're in some deep shit. You must have done somethin' really stupid."

"Right," I said, waiting to hear him out.

"If you want to help me unload this trailer, I'll pay you fifty dollars."

"You're on," I said.

When we arrived in Orlando I helped him unload the furniture and it turned out being a lot of work. It's amazing how much furniture can be crammed into one of those trailers. We had to be careful to not damage anything. We finished the job; he paid me, and dropped me off at a gas station on the edge of Orlando. He was heading back north for another load of snowbird's furniture.

Chastity answered on the second ring. "Hi, Chastity, I'm in Orlando. Come back to me," I said, cramming it all in before she had a chance to hang up.

"How did you get in Florida?"

"I hitchhiked."

"You're crazy, crazy."

"Come back to me."

"No. You love your stupid friends and alcohol more than you love me."

"Chastity, please, take me back." I started crying and we had to wait for a while until I got control. "I have changed. I promise. I have changed."

"Changed?"

"Yeah, changed, I've quit drinking, forever, completely quit."

"Ha, what a laugh."

"It's true, believe me. This has been a nightmare. I miss you, baby. Please take me back. I'll work like a crazy man, but mostly I'll love you like you deserve."

"You've lied to me, over and over."

"I know, but I'm not lying this time. I really have quit drinking."

"What about your friends that you love so much?"

"We're not in Utah anymore. I don't have any friends."

"Wherever we went, you'd find new friends and leave me by myself. I know you!"

"No, no I wouldn't. If I find new friends I'll make them second-fiddle to you. I'll never abandon you again. Remember how close and loving we were in the beginning? It can be like that again. I promise, because I do love you. Come back to me."

Chastity began crying. "I've always loved you too, you know that, but you're flawed, badly flawed. Honestly, Justin, I don't have the strength to handle any more heartache."

"There'll be none, I promise."

There was a long pause while she thought about it and there was some more crying, on both of our parts.

"All right, Justin. I'll give you one more chance. You really have quit drinkin'?"

"Cross my heart and hope to die."

"Let me remind you of something about marriage, it comes with responsibilities . . . lot's of responsibilities. You do get that?"

"Yeah, of course."

"Oh, I must be out of my mind . . . but yeah . . . yeah . . . I'll take you back. Uh, I'll pack a couple bags and I'll be waiting for you out in my parent's gazebo, it's in front and to the left." Then she gave me her address.

"Yippee. You won't regret it. I promise. Oh, do you have wheels?"

"Yeah, an old Volkswagen bug," she said.

"Will it make it all the way to Kanab, Utah? I want to go there and find work, maybe teach school. I couldn't help it, while I outlined the plans that would bond us together for the rest of our lives, I cried like a baby. I was so relieved, so happy she had given me another shot. I would never mess up again, never.

"The car? I don't know. It has a hundred and ten thousand miles on it."

"It'll make it."

"Kanab, Utah, wow! Are you sure?"

"I've never been more sure of anything in my life. Do you have any money?" I asked.

"Yeah, yeah, I guess I could handle Kanab." she said, trying to take it all in.

"Do you have money?" I repeated.

"Money? Yeah, money? I have two hundred dollars. I just got paid. I've been working in the costume department for Disney here in Orlando."

"Good. I'll have about forty bucks to add to the pot."

"Okay, but you're not bringin' much into this 'second chance' gift I'm giving you, are you?"

"I'm bringing more than you think. I'm bringing the new me, and that's worth a whole shit load."

"Yeah, well, we'll see."

"What time?" I asked.

"Eleven o'clock, because Mom and Dad will be asleep by then." Then she gave me her parent's address.

"Why're we meeting at the gazebo?" I asked.

"Because Mom and Dad hate your guts. In fact, if Dad were to see you, he might take a notion to shoot you."

"Gotcha."

Chastity is the main focus of my life these days, the only focus really. She runs a little antique shop, *Chastity's Antiques,* in Kanab, and she is one of the best marathoners in the state of Utah. Actually, she has a goal to run a marathon in every state in the union. So we travel a lot to attend marathons in all 50 states that comprises this great nation. I write books on travel, so these trips benefit us both. Our life together is like a dream, really, consisting of all sorts of writing and running.

I love Chastity to distraction. During these trips we find a perfect balance: she runs and I research and write. Fortunately, we have enough money to close up our home on the outskirts of Kanab, nestled in the beautiful red Canyonlands, and hit the road in our Winnebago Chieftain. How can we afford to do this? Well, I've made absolutely insane amounts of money writing about travel, and *Chastity's Antiques* hasn't done too shabby either. I can't believe I am actually making a living as a writer, who would've thunk? But make no mistake; writing is a brutal racket, competitive as all hell, and cutthroat, wow, cutthroat. "Writing is the hardest way earning a living, with the possible exception of wrestling alligators."—Olin Miller. At first I tried my hand at writing thrillers, but nobody found them all that thrilling. So I changed up and concentrated on writing about travel. When you break it all down, I am proud that I have been able to provide Chastity with those niceties in life she so richly deserves. After all in those early days she did have to put up with a scoundrel.

We've been reunited for five years now and soon we are going to bring a little girl into the world, this according to a recent ultrasound. Being pregnant has wreaked havoc with Chastity's training schedule, but she says it will be worth it in the end because she believes the little girl is going to be a world-class marathoner, an Olympian even. Chastity says she'll start training our baby girl as soon as she can walk. Actually I'm a little conflicted about training a mere toddler. But, actually, I think Chastity is just having fun messing with my head. But it really doesn't matter because my love for Chastity will remain steadfast, immutable.

EMERGENCE

A fully bloomed saltwort plant, a species of salsola, broke away from its taproot and began tumbling. The saltwort had been in flaxseed brought in by Ukrainian farmers in the mid-19th century, they had accidentally introduced the hearty plant to American soil. The wind tumbled the saltwort plant through Wolf Creek Pass, Utah, then on through the North Fork of the Duchesne River region. It spread seeds all along its path, as was Mother Nature's intent. But eventually it got hung up in a thicket of oak brush just inside the city limits of Tabiona, Utah, and there it took a decade-long rest; it turned sere and became a tumbleweed as it waited.

After the long-time inactivity, a gust of hot wind slammed into it and dislodged it from its resting place, sending it rolling along the land.

It careened along Highway 35 that runs from Hanna, Utah, to the intersection of Highway 87. Then it tumbled along until it entered Tabiona's Main Street, where it continued rolling briskly along, driven by a ferocious windstorm with great volumes of boiling dust. It skittered by a general store, a post office, a saloon, a Mormon church, and a small gas station. In fact, in just a few minutes, it nearly completed passage through the entire business district, but before it could complete that passage it got hung up again in the two-by-four bracings of a pole supporting a sign that read Folksbury's Barber Shop. It was here that it took another protracted rest.

The barbershop was a fifteen-by-fifteen-foot rude frame building painted eggshell white; it had one door and two windows. The shop was illuminated by a single, bare incandescent light bulb hanging from a frayed light cord.

The light was on because of dust choking off the sun and seeping into the shop, then flitting about on what had formerly been invisible currents of air.

Two people occupied the shop, Adam and Garth Folksbury, father and son. Both coughed a few times from the irritating dust particles. The howling wind played on the Folksbury's nerves, long since as taut as over-tuned banjo strings. They desperately needed a customer in order to earn enough money to buy badly needed food.

"Will ya listen to that wind?" Adam asked Garth, watching his son sweep a floor that scarcely needed it—it had been some time since the floor had been covered with hair clippings.

They were hoping to cut a head of hair, anybody's head of hair. They had been eating nothing but potatoes for nearly a week. But the prospects weren't good. Most everybody in those parts was barely surviving and mostly spent their money on necessities.

"That wind is scary," Garth said. "Will it blow the barbershop down?"

"Uh, no, that would take a hurricane, or the big bad wolf," Adam said, laughing.

Garth managed just the slightest of smiles at his father's attempt at humor. Laughter didn't come easy for the boy, and hadn't for some time. "I sure would like something good to eat tonight, besides just plain ol' potatoes," he said, his eyes filling with tears.

Adam watched his son trying to be manly and get control of his emotions, and it hurt seeing it. "I'm gonna cut someone's hair today, I promise, and then we're gonna have ourselves a good rabbit stew with all sorts of vegetables."

"Yeah, that's great." Garth shook his head of wild red hair, darker in the poor light shrouded by the windstorm; in good sunlight his hair glowed with copper-colored tints. He was nine years old and had been home-schooled; he'd never set foot in a public school. His mother, Dolores, had done a satisfactory job with his education, considering she only had an eleventh-grade education herself, she decided not to finish high school. "But we don't have a rabbit for the stew," Garth said, wiping at the tears.

"I know, but what say we hunt us down one of them lop-eared varmints this afternoon, if this danged wind lets up? I've got five .22 caliber shells that should be enough to do the job."

"Yeah . . . that would be good."

"But I'll cut a head of hair today, too, just you watch, and we'll have us some vegetables."

The radio was tuned into KLO, broadcast out of Ogden, Utah. Adam, an unusually slender man with a bald head, a prominent Adam's apple, and long, gangly arms and legs, settled back in his barber's chair and relaxed. "Do you want to listen to one of your radio programs? I have a newspaper here to keep me contented until a customer shows."

"Yeah, Pa, I want to listen to Fibber McGee and Molly."

Adam Folksbury sat in his barber chair and began reading an article about the economy in a week-old issue of the *Salt Lake Tribune*, dated August 13, 1938. It said that a gallon of gasoline had gone up to ten cents, that a loaf of bread was nine cents, and that Americans were paying thirteen cents for a loaf of bread. He thought the prices were an outrage.

Garth stayed nearby in a customer's chair and listened to an old Crosley 48 Widget radio on a small catch-all table. He laughed occasionally at the Fibber and Molly's jokes.

Adam smiled, hearing Garth laugh; there hadn't been much of that lately, at least in his household, and that went back nearly ten years. It went back to when the United States economy had exploded into a financial convulsion on that infamous Black Tuesday in 1929. Adam, twenty years old at the time, had just finished barbering school over in Salt Lake. He had been born and raised in Duchesne, Utah. In fact, after barbering school he moved back to Duchesne and became a barber's apprentice there in a small shop with a fellow named Ricky Nichols.

He met Dolores in Duchesne during that apprenticeship. Dolores had just dropped out of high school over in Heber, she had quit just after completing the 11th grade. Dolores was in Duchesne visiting a girlfriend. She ended up spending more time with Adam than her girlfriend. He talked her into marrying him and moving to Tabiona, where he would open his own shop and provide her with a comfortable standard of living, at least that had been the plan.

The wind howled through Tabiona. Adam nodded off to sleep, a small respite from the gnawing anxiety that he was coming up short as a provider for a household of three. The country was at the tail end of the Depression, and he should be making more money; he was afraid their poverty was more his fault than the fault of economic downturn. He'd been stupid and stubborn, hanging on to the barbershop, which had been a losing proposition from the get-go. He just kept on thinking it would pay, but it never had. There were 150 people in Tabiona proper and several hundred more in the outlying regions, ample numbers to keep a barbershop busy, moderately speaking, but nobody wanted to spend money at his barbershop, apparently. The people were spending their money for more important items. If it hadn't been for his wife, Dolores, they would have starved. She had a little sewing business that kept a meager amount of victuals on their table.

Adam started in with a gentle snoring and Garth continued listening to the radio.

Then the unexpected happened . . . the little bell tinkled and in walked a customer.

"How ya doin' Adam?" a short, stocky fellow named Henry Nash asked.

"Uh, Henry, I can't complain," Adam said, rubbing his eyes.

"Sorry to interrupt your snooze, but I need shorn; it's either that or a dog license."

"Glad to do 'er, Henry, climb aboard," Adam said, climbing down from the barber's chair.

"Hello, young feller. You the helper today?" Henry asked Garth.

"Yeah, sir, Mr. Nash, and I bet I could shave you with Dad's straightedge razor, if you're a-needin' it."

Nash threw his cowboy hat on the table and laughed. "Naw, I think I'll let your father do the straightedge work, if you don't mind. But I appreciate the offer."

Adam Folksbury laughed and looked at Garth. "Uh, you just keep thumbing through that comic book. You're not gonna shave anybody today, leastwise with a straightedge." Adam looked at Henry. "How do you want your hair?"

"Cut," Henry said.

The wind howled outside the little barbershop and the air seemed to have an electric charge to it. It felt to Garth like the fine little hairs on his arms and legs were standing on end, but he thought he must just be imagining it. He started looking through the pages of an Action Comic Book that had a picture of Superman on the cover holding up an old-time green automobile over his head, bashing the front end of it on a boulder. The bad guys, who'd likely been dislodged from the car, were running for the hills with their mouths wide open. The comic book had been thumbed through so many times it was frayed. Garth had several others as well, falling apart from being read so many times.

"Money's a bit tight these days, Adam," Henry commented. "Would you accept a chunk of beef for the barberin'?"

"Yeah, that saves me havin' to hunt down a hop rabbit for the stew pot."

"My cattle operation is doin' poorly and I'm cash poor. Nobody's buyin'."

"A good bit of this country's still in a bad way, ain't it?"

"If you think we're in bad shape here in central Utah, how would you like being one of them Okies living out there in the Dust Bowl? They been hit with a double whammy these days, the danged depression and the danged Dust Bowl. And, if war breaks out in Europe . . . it will be a triple whammy."

"It seems to me we have our own Dust Bowl out there today."

"That wind is a doozy, isn't it? I left the old lady over at Marge's General Store with a dollar in her fist, and then I headed over here. I'd trouble finding your shop in this danged wind, and it's a straight shot."

"Hard to believe," Adam said, shaking his head, clipping steadily.

"I was over by Fruitland the other day and one of them Okies was in the gas station trying to trade an old carpenter's plane for gas. He was on his way to California to pick fruit."

"Did he succeed, trading for the gas?"

"No, that old bag that runs that joint run him out. She's an ornery ol' heifer. 'Get on into Heber,' she said, 'someone there might need a carpenter's plane, but I don't, and why in tarnation would I?' 'Don't knows that I'll make Heber with what little gas I have,' the man said as he slouched toward his ol' jalopy."

"What'd them Okies look like?" Adam asked.

"They were a sight for sore eyes. They had everything they owned hanging all over their ol' jalopy, and they were dirty and ragged."

"What a shame. When they get to California they probably won't get hired-on picking fruit. I hear tell there ain't enough fruit pickin' jobs to go 'round."

"Yeah," Nash said, "I feel sorry for 'em."

"Did you talk to 'em?"

"No, didn't figure there was much use to it."

"Yeah."

"I thought about buying them gas outa my own pocket, but thought better of it."

"Yeah."

"The fellow had his ol' lady and six kids. I don't know how in thunder they all managed to get into that ol' jalopy."

"It must have been uncomfortable riding all the way out here from Oklahoma."

"Yeah. Adam, the danged country is going to hell in a hand basket."

"Ain't it just."

"Did you listen to the Joe Louis-Max Schmeling fight?"

"No, when was it?"

"Just this last June. I think it was on the twenty-second."

"I was down Heber way back about that time."

"It was some fight."

"What happened? I haven't bothered keeping up with stuff like that lately."

"Louis knocked him out in the first round."

"Hey, how 'bout that?"

"Yeah! So much for Hitler's Aryan Supremacy crap."

"Sure enough. And Schmeling was the symbol of Nazi Germany. Leastwise, that's what was being said."

"Yeah, some symbol. What took you down Heber way?"

Adam was working a pair of scissors and they were going snick-snick-snick as he trimmed the top of Nash's head. He would grab up a handful of Nash's hair and that hair poking up between his fingers got lopped off with the scissors. While he snipped, the wind continued howling. "I was looking for work," Adam said.

"What sorta work?"

"With the Bureau of Reclamation."

"What are they doin' down that way?"

"Puttin' in an earthen dam across the Provo River just below Charleston."

"What in thunder for?"

"They're gonna build the Deer Creek Reservoir."

"Haven't heard tell of this-un."

"Yeah, they're gonna have an electric plant there at the dam site."

"I'm not so sure it is such a good idea to flood that good bottom land in there below Charleston. That's some purty country, sitting there at the base of Mount Timpanogas."

"A lot of homes are going underwater, sheep ranches, cattle ranches, roads, gardens, barns, sheds."

"A shame."

"Yeah, a shame, but I could sure use the work. I'm at the end of my tether, Henry."

"Buck up, Adam; things are bound to get better. I take it the Bureau of Reclamation didn't hire you?"

"No. They said I was too thin to hold up under the strain of the hard work that would be required."

"Sorry, Adam."

"It don't make no never mind, Henry. Nah, don't fret none over it, I've figgered a way out of this mess."

"Good for you; if it works, let me know. I'd really like to eat something 'sides beef. Right now the ol' lady and I can't afford anything else, so we're eating up our stock, and believe it or not, a feller can get tired of steak."

"My plan can't fail," Adam said. "But I doubt you'd be wantin' to follow my lead."

"Hey, there, now, Adam," Nash craned his head around to take a look at his old acquaintance.

But Adam placed both hands on Nash's head and gently turned it back around, acting like the need to finish the haircut was a priority. "Hold still; do you want one of your danged ears lopped off?"

Henry let his head be turned back to the forward position, but it didn't ease his mind. He wondered what Adam had meant by what he'd said. Finally, Nash shook off the disturbing thoughts and veered off onto another subject. "I read in the *Tribune* that Congress signed a new bill called the Agricultural Adjustment Act, or something like that."

"What's that?" Adam asked.

"I'm not sure, but it was designed to give help to those poor Dust Bowl farmers."

"Probably won't help much . . . government always falls short on its promises."

"I don't imagine it will work. Wish't they'd write some relief act for Utahans."

The shingle off a local citizen's nearby roof smacked the sign post out in front of the barbershop

"The wind's tearin' things up," Adam noted.

"So it would seem."

"Gasoline has gone up to ten cents a gallon."

"Highway robbery. Those blasted oil companies are gouging us again."

"Yeah, the minimum wage is a lousy twenty-five cents an hour. Takes nearly a half hour of work to put a stinkin' gallon of gas in my ol' heap."

"If the price keeps going up, we're going to have to go back to the horse and buggy."

"Ain't that the truth."

Adam finished the haircut and put a hand mirror up to Henry's face so he could see the barbering job.

"Yeah, it's cut, it sure 'nough is," Henry said.

Adam pulled the protective sheet off Henry, shook it out and placed it on a hook. Then he unfastened the protective collar that had kept hair clippings from dribbling down Henry's neck. Next, he tipped up a bottle of tonic and shook a liberal amount out on top of Nash's head, then he kneaded the freshly cut hair, took a comb, parted it on one side and fashioned it into a pleasing style.

The air was redolent with the scent of the tonic, a smell that Garth would forever associate with his father and the little barbershop on Main Street there in Tabiona, Utah.

Lastly, Adam took a little whisk brush and swept the trimmings from Henry's clothing.

Henry stood up and put on his Stetson. "See ya, Adam," he said.

"See ya, Henry, and thanks for the business."

"It was my pleasure. I'll put that hunk of beef in your Ford. It's freshly kilt, but you need to get 'er chilled down 'fore long."

"I'll do 'er, thank you."

Henry stood up, ruffled Garth's hair and said. "I wish't I had a strapping young lad like you to work on my ranch."

"Gee, Dad, could I go work for Mr. Henry? I just betcha I could learn to ranch in no time at all."

"No son, not just yet; you're a little young for it."

The men laughed and Henry left the shop.

When Adam and Garth drove home, the ferocious wind had mostly died away, but there was still a warm breeze filtering through town. The town smelled musty, like the inside of a potato cellar; untold cubic yards of central Utah dirt had blown through during the storm. The earthy smell had replaced the stale smell of unwashed bodies entrenched in the car's upholstery, and the pungent odor of raw gasoline and motor oil that was always present in and about the Model T. The new smell almost seemed like an improvement. As they drove, they were tuned into KLO on the car radio. Tommy Dorsey and his band was playing "Taking a Chance on Love."

"Do you like that lovey-dovey music? I like Roy Rogers' songs best. He's the king of the cowboys."

Adam laughed. "Yeah, I like that lovey-dovey music, but Roy Rogers' songs are okay, too."

When father and son arrived at the tarpaper shack called home, Dolores Folksbury was sitting at a roughly hewn kitchen table made from planking. She was wearing a threadbare housedress, and sewing on another dress.

"Hi, little fellow," Dolores said, putting a big set of green eyes on her little man. She had red/orange hair the color of begonias; freckles were splattered all over her exposed skin; she was thin, wispy, and short in stature; her hips were narrow and her breasts were underdeveloped, but she was, in spite of it all, rather attractive. She was only in her late twenties, but she had little crows feet radiating out from her eyes. She looked worn; like a person gets who's been to war.

"Hi," Garth said. "We've got beef."

"Wonderful! You fellows did a good job. God knows we need something today besides potatoes. Were you a good little boy today?"

"I was an angel," Garth said.

Everybody laughed. "He was well-behaved today," Adam said. "He even offered to help with the haircut I gave Henry Nash that earned us the beef. He offered to shave Nash with my straightedge."

"God forbid," Dolores said, and then they had a laugh over it.

It felt strange to them—laughing, that is—there hadn't been much of it lately.

Dolores pointed to some purple cloth on the table. "Marge wants this dress sewed up by tonight. She's going to a movie over in Roosevelt."

"Purple?"

"Passion purple," Dolores said.

"Yikes."

"Yeah," Dolores said, "and she wants a tunic with a gathered V-neck. A tunic, imagine."

"Is that what big city women are wearin' these days?"

"I don't know. But look at this cloth, it's a new material to the market named polyester/rayon . . . it's fifty-five percent polyester and forty-five percent rayon. I'm not sure it will hold up under wear 'n' tear. But it's what the woman wanted."

"Are you gonna get 'er done in time, so you can pick up some vegetables at her general store?"

"I think so, if you two will stop yacking. What kind of beef did Nash give you?"

"It's a shank with the brisket attached. It should keep us goin', for a couple days anyway."

"I need to finish up this dress and get it over to Marge's. Would you get the stew going, Adam, and I'll finish this up and go fetch us some vegetables."

"Okay, Dolores. I'll get some of the beef boiling right away, we can rustle us up a terrific stew."

"Is there any gas in the heap?"

"Enough to get you over to Marge's General Store and back. But can you stop at the station and put in about three gallons with your dress-making money? The heap needs fuel."

"I'm sure it does. How else would you get to the barbershop so you can sit there and stare at the four walls?"

"Marge, please. Don't start in on me. I can't take it—not tonight of all nights. It's very important that we get along tonight . . . very important."

"Oh, really, why?"

"You'll soon know, Dolores, you'll soon know."

"Oh, really? A rich uncle is leaving us money?" Dolores asked, sneering.

Garth was fearful of what was coming . . . a shouting match. It happened all the time. So he stormed off to his room to play with a top his father had carved out of Englemann spruce. Garth toyed with the top for a while, spinning it on an unvarnished plank floor and listened for another flare up from his parents, but it didn't come. Imagine that. When his parents quarreled it scared him. He relaxed and turned on a cheap little radio he'd gotten for Christmas, sent to him by his grandmother. The first thing that came up was a man peddling Old Dutch Cleanser. The man said the cleanser "chases dirt" that it "gets down to work in preserving time." Then Heber J. Grant, the seventh president of the Latter-Day-Saints Church came on the air. He was talking about some stake he'd dedicated up near Logan, Utah. The solemn ceremony had been attended by five members of the Quorum of the Twelve. But before long he was called to supper.

The stew had to be the best food Garth had ever eaten. All of them ate until they were stuffed.

The next morning Garth was brought abruptly awake by a horrible screeching that started out low and guttural, and then built up to an ear-piercing crescendo. It was the sort of agonized scream that will stand one's hair on end.

It was hard to tell at first, but he came to realize that it was coming from his mother. It was coming from the rear of the house, back by the shed. He rushed back there, not taking time to get dressed. His mother came rushing out of the shed and caught him up in her arms in a hug that almost smothered him. Her tears wet his shoulder.

"What's wrong?"

"Don't go in the shed! Don't even go near the shed!"

"Why?"

"It's your father . . . He's dead."

"Dead?"

"Dead."

"What happened?" he asked, as the tears began spilling down his face. "Dead?" Having said that, he tried slipping past her to get into the shed. But she caught him by his long johns and hauled him back.

They returned to the house and Dolores caught Garth up in her arms again and they hung onto each other and cried long and hard and openly. It was a cleansing thing. Then they both turned the spigot off and seemed to be done with it, the crying. It was time to take action, to go for the law. Both climbed into the Model T and went for the sheriff.

They returned with the sheriff trailing in his '38 Buick four-door sedan. It was black and white and it had a sign on the front doors that read, "Duchesne County Sheriff's Department." The sheriff was fat. He obviously hadn't been affected a great deal by America's economic downturn. Dolores and the sheriff disappeared around back and before long they came back up front.

"There's nothing we can do for him, nothing," the sheriff said. "What a shame, what a shame. Why would a man do such a thing?"

Dolores wanted to tell the fat sheriff that Adam hadn't been eating too well, nor had his family. She wanted to compare Adam's spare frame with the sheriff's fat frame, but she decided it would serve no purpose. "He's been feeling beat down," she finally allowed.

"I'll call ol' Jeb Jacobsen, the undertaker over in Roosevelt and have Adam hauled into the funeral home."

"Okay."

"Now I'd suggest we sit down and handle the death documents," the sheriff said.

"Come in, come in. Yeah, let's get it handled," Dolores said.

While they worked on the paperwork, Garth ran around the house and burst into the shed. Adam Folksbury was hanging from a ceiling rafter. He had hung himself with an old lariat. A beam of sunlight filtered into the shed and dust motes and small particles of alfalfa from nearby hay bales flitted about in the disturbed air. His father's face was a vivid purple and his eyes were open and registering nothing. The intelligence and life itself had been stricken from his once lively eyes. His father's bladder and bowels had vacated their contents and the inside of the shed held a powerful stench.

Garth had never known hell, but he figured he was probably as close to it as he would ever get. He lunged out of the shed and had himself another long cry. He thought his heart would break. But before long he went back in the house, his face smudged with tears, sat down politely and listened to his mother and the sheriff conduct the business concerning his father's death.

He sat there quietly, thinking about what was to become of him and his mother. He could scarcely believe it. His father was gone . . . no more hunting trips . . . no more talks on all manner of subjects . . . no more wrestling and fooling around . . . no more hugs . . . none of that, never again. He had never been so profoundly sad.

"Why did Dad have to go and kill himself like that?"

"He must have been terribly sad."

"Well, God shouldn't have let him do it. God's mean."

"Gracious sakes, don't say that! Do you want us to get struck by lightning or something?"

"No, I'm sorry. I'm just so sad, Ma."

"I know, honey, I know. I'm sad, too. But we won't be sad forever. I just bet you before long we'll both be happy as a lark."

"Are larks happy?"

"I've heard tell they are."

Three days later they put Adam in the ground in a tiny cemetery on the outskirts of Tabiona. Adam hadn't been the only suicide from gnawing poverty there in Tabiona. One other father of a family of six had shot himself just six months earlier. Anyway, when the first shovel full of dirt and pebbles splattered onto Adam's coffin, Dolores and Garth cried again momentarily, but when they were finished, they never cried for Adam again. There was a hollow place in their hearts, yes, but they were done with the crying. It was time to put the past behind them.

The next morning Dolores and Garth Folksbury loaded the Model T Ford Roadster, filling all the available space, including the rumble seat, with their most important household items. The rest of the property was left to Jeb Jacobsen, the undertaker. Dolores gave it all to him in lieu of cash money for the burial services.

Dolores hadn't told Garth about her decision to pull up stakes and move in with her aged mother in Keetley, Utah, some 100 miles northwest of Tabiona. So Garth was surprised when suddenly he found himself helping load the car.

"Where are we going?" he asked.

"To live with my mother in Keetley."

"I don't want to live with her! She's old!"

"Gracious sakes, Garth, we don't have a choice. How would you like starving to death?"

"What about my friends, Johnny and Billy Baumgartner?"

"What about them?"

"Will I ever see them again?"

"Of course you will. You'll come back here someday . . . someday when you learn to drive."

"Okay. Okay, but what about our horse, Ol' Brindle? What about the stuff in the house and shed?"

"It all belongs to the undertaker now, the old thief. But it's not all bad. Ol' Brindle will finally get some oats and hay, he won't have to forage all over Duchesne County just to stay alive."

The Model T was a 1927 model and it had a 2.9 liter engine that was tired out and hard to start. Adam Folksbury had bought it second-hand for a song; it had been a high-mileage taxi over in Salt Lake. Dolores retarded the spark with a lever on the dash and then she turned the stubborn old crank on the front of the engine. She spun the crank until she was tired and gasping for air, but it didn't want to start. She rested and then tried it again, making certain she kept her thumb and face out of harm's way in case the old thing backfired. Untold numbers of American citizens had had their thumbs and faces broken by Henry Ford's Model T's.

The Folksbury's Ford was manufactured the last year old Henry Ford produced the Model T. "You can have any color you want, just so it's black," Henry had said. Actually, the Folksbury's Model T was copper, exceptions were made in later production years.

Dolores finally got the engine started and they were off. When the Model T climbed out onto Highway 40, the frame flexed and the car groaned in seeming protest. Dolores sighed and pointed the Model T's nose toward Keetley and urged it to higher speeds.

"I'm scared," Garth said as he wiped away the tears. He was being uprooted from the only home he had ever known.

"So am I, Garth, so am I," Dolores said as she manipulated three pedals on the floor and a lever on the dash to change the planetary gear into the second and highest gear. The old roadster wheezed and protested against being forced to go faster.

A jackrabbit broke out onto the highway in front of them and the right front wheel passed over it. The Model T made a perceptible lurch and they heard a *thudk*, but neither remarked about the fate of the careless rabbit; their thoughts were fully occupied with what lay ahead.

Dolores had managed to buy two gallons of gasoline the day before, but that wasn't going to be enough to make the journey, and she was completely broke. She had, however, managed to bring thick slices of roast beef and a few fresh vegetables.

It was a hot day and the pavement ahead looked squiggly with heat waves.

A mule deer bounded along a hillside to their right. It looked to be a two-point buck.

The interior of the roadster was sweltering hot. The sun sat high in the powder-blue sky and not a single cloud was there to interfere with its intensity. They had the windows down, but it didn't help.

"How many people live in Keetley?"

"Fifteen."

"When we were there last Christmas, I didn't see fifteen people."

"Well, there are fifteen people."

"Good, they won't have a danged schoolhouse, then."

"Ha! You'll be going to school all right, over in Heber. They have two grade schools over there. The home-schoolin' days are over. There're three thousand people in Heber; you should make lotsa nice friends."

Steam began to pour out of the old roadster's radiator.

"Oh, no, the engine has overheated and we haven't even traveled twenty miles."

"Is that bad?"

"Yeah, that's bad."

Dolores got out and retrieved a large canvas bag she'd hung on the radiator support rod. She removed the radiator cap carefully so as not to get scalded, and poured fresh water into the radiator. The old roadster had been low on water. She hadn't checked it before they departed. Adam had always handled that sort of thing.

She walked around to Garth's side window. "Do you want a drink of water?"

He took the bag, tipped it up, and took a small drink. Dolores did the same, then she replaced the canvas bag on the radiator support rod and they were off.

Before long they reached Fruitland and she pulled into the little gas station there in hopes of getting at least one gallon of gas. That was all she needed to complete their journey on into Heber, where she hoped to attain a little more gas that would take them all the way to Keetley. She could only hope to attain a gallon at a time. She didn't know how she was going to pull it off, but she simply had to have the gas.

She pulled up to the gas pump, climbed out of the roadster and headed toward the station's door. An old dog of 57-or-so-different-varieties bared its teeth and growled at her.

June Rex, proprietor, stepped from the station with a cigarette dangling from the side of her mouth. "Shut your yap you miserable cur or I'll kick out a couple of your teeth." she told the snarling dog. The dog shut up and drifted back off to sleep. "What'll it be, ma'am?"

"Hi, uh, ma'am. Uh, I need just one gallon of gas so I can make it on in to Heber."

"Is that right? Big spender, huh?"

"Well, here's the thing. I don't actually have any money."

"Well, then, you aren't actually goin' to get any gas then, are ya?"

"I was wondering if you'd accept an old radio in trade?"

"Got a radio."

"How about a set of encyclopedias?"

"Don't read much."

"How about—"

"Scram, girlie! It's simple: If you don't have cash money, you're not getting gas. You must be one of them danged Okies that's comin' through here all the time."

"No, I'm not, you horrible old woman. I'm from Tabiona. Have a heart. My husband just died—"

"Makes no never mind to me who died. Now scram before I set ol' Chester on ya." She looked at the cur.

"You horrible ol' woman," Dolores said as she climbed back into the car.

"Gee, Ma, what's wrong, you're kinda crying? How come you didn't get any gas?"

"That horrible old woman wouldn't take anything in trade."

"Why didn't you just give her money for the gas?"

"Because I don't have any."

"So are we gonna run out of gas?"

"Yeah."

"So what's goin' to happen?"

"I don't know, but we are goin' to make it to Keetley, if we have to crawl."

"I don't want to crawl, Ma."

Dolores wiped away the tears and chuckled a little.

Before long they topped out on the Daniel's Canyon Summit and started rolling downhill toward beautiful Heber Valley. The Model T's engine was running quite strongly, but she shut it off and coasted for several miles to save gas. Finally, because she was worried the brakes might be overheating, she put it in the highest gear, popped the clutch and started the engine by compression. That saved her from having to stop and go through the task of spinning the crank.

The model T coughed like an ancient cart horse and then went silent altogether and coasted to a stop.

"Are we going to have to sleep in the car?"

"No, I don't think so."

They rolled up to the entry to Lodgepole Campground. She could have continued coasting a ways, the road still went steeply downhill, but she was afraid of losing the brakes and letting the Model T get away from her. They had already lost part of the family; it would be senseless to risk the remaining members.

Dolores got out and opened the hood to alert motorists that she was having a problem.

Five minutes later a U.S. Forest Service agent pulled out of the campground. He rolled up in a green forest service pickup, stepped out, and walked to her. "Car trouble, ma'am?" he asked. He was a large man with just the slightest hint of fat around his midriff. He had coal black hair and his skin was bronzed by the sun. He was all decked out in a forest service uniform. Dolores thought him quite handsome in a rugged sort of way.

"Well, yeah, I've run out of gas," Dolores said.

He turned and went back to his pickup and pulled out a Jerry Can strapped firmly to the pickup bed with tie downs, walked back with the can and poured a couple gallons of gas into the Model T, returned to his pickup and strapped the Jerry Can firmly back into place. "Where ya headed, ma'am?" he asked.

"Keetley, and I haven't got a dime to my name. I can't pay you for that gas you just dumped into my car, not right now, anyway."

"I ain't asking for money. This here gas was paid for by the federal government. I'll have the forest service take forty cents out of my next paycheck. The gas is my gift to you."

"I'll pay you as soon as I get money, regardless. Do you live in Heber?"

"Forget it, ma'am, really. What's your name? My name is Elroy Winterton."

"Dolores Folksbury."

"Well, Dolores, pleased to meet you. Where are you headed?"

"To Keetley. Garth and me." She pointed to her son. "We're moving in with my mother out there."

"Well, Miss Folksbury, you could make it up to me by frying me up a batch of chicken over there in Keetley. But that wouldn't be right and proper, if there's a Mr. Folksbury?" He looked at her ring finger, but there was no ring. She had temporarily removed it for fear of loosing it during the move.

"There isn't. My husband died four days ago."

"I'm so sorry to hear that," he said.

"I could cook you some chicken, but you ain't one of them fellows that tries taking advantage of a woman, are you? You know, a wolf?" She immediately felt foolish. Why had she asked such a ridiculous question? The guy was probably just lookin' for a chicken dinner, wasn't he?

"No, ma'am, I'm not a wolf," Elroy said, laughing. "I am simply a man wanting to eat a chicken dinner and have a conversation with an attractive, red-headed woman—get to know her, you know? Is that so wrong?"

"No, no, of course not," Dolores said, her face turning crimson.

"Well?"

"Well, what?"

"Do I get the chicken dinner or not?" he asked, eyes twinkling.

"Yeah, Elroy, yeah, I suppose. But don't call on me for another six months . . . that should give me enough time to heal after the loss of my husband."

"Six months it is. What's your mother's name over there in Keetley?"

"Helen Osyka. Thank you so much for the gas."

"My pleasure, ma'am. Howdy, young feller," he said, looking at Adam.

"Howdy," Garth said.

Elroy climbed into his forest service pickup and drove away. A gust of wind came rushing down Daniel's Canyon, a sudden burst of it, and rustled the leaves on the nearby aspen. They made a dry, rasping sound and sparkles of light danced about on the leaves, all lit by a bright, noonday sun. Dolores rolled the Model T down the hill, let out the clutch and started the engine by compression. It started on the first try and she let out a huge sigh of relief.

When they rolled into the yard in Keetley, the elderly Osyka was sitting on the porch in her panties and bra, sipping iced tea. Her once elegant, two-story frame home with mansard roof, needed paint and shingles. The lawn had given way to foxtails, dandelions, and cheat grass.

Dolores climbed out of the Model T and walked up to the porch. "Mother, what in the world? You just can't sit out here in your underwear."

Helen Osyka fixed a set of mean little eyes on Dolores. "And just who in hell are you to tell me what I can or cannot do? Get on out of here."

"What the world? I'm Dolores, your daughter."

"Bullshit, I never had any children. I don't much care for them."

"What?"

"Who's this little snotnose?" the old lady asked, pointing a gnarled, arthritic finger at Garth, standing by his mother.

"What a thing to say to a child. He's your grandson. Don't you recognize him?"

"Oh, ha, I very much doubt it. Look at the homely little bugger. He's no kin of mine."

Tears spilled from Garth's eyes and he ran back to the Model T.

"That was a damned mean thing to say about your only grandson. You should be ashamed."

"To hell with him. To hell with you, too, whoever you are."

Dolores had had enough. She pulled Helen Osyka to her feet and marched her into the house and began dressing her . . . enough was enough.

"You bitch!" Helen screamed. "You can't just come into my home like this, like you own the goddamn place!" She let out a long, wailing screech and when Dolores bent over to help with her shoes, Helen tried to claw her face with her long, yellowed fingernails. But Dolores saw it coming and got out of the way. "Who are you? Get out!" the old lady screeched.

"I am your *daughter*, Dolores. Don't you remember? I called you on the phone a couple days ago. Your grandson, Garth, and I are moving in. We don't have any place to go. Remember, Adam killed himself a few days ago."

"What a story. Young lady, whoever you are, you really should get some help. I think you are seriously disturbed."

Dolores laughed at that one, then turned to a less serious matter. "When did you start using such offensive language?"

"What the hell's it to you? Get out." She tried to kick Dolores on the shin.

That was it, Dolores slapped the old lady across the face.. There is nothing quite like a good slap to the kisser to clear up a scattered mind, and it worked wonderfully.

The old lady shook her head a little, then said, "Dolores, baby girl, it is you, isn't it?" She gave Dolores a big hug and enfolded her in her arms. "Why in the world would you slap an old lady in the face like that?"

"It's a long story."

"Where's Garth, that sweet little feller of yours?"

"In the car."

"In the car? Why would you leave him in the car? He'll have a heat stroke. Bring him in here, this minute."

Dolores stepped onto the porch and motioned for Garth to come in. When he walked into the living room his face was streaked with tears.

"Why are you crying, young man? Probably because you're overheated, right? Sometimes your mother just doesn't use good sense. Come here and give me a big hug and let me see you." Garth sidled forward to receive his hug, then his grandmother stepped back to get a good look at him. "My, my, look at you. Look how you've grown, and you're such a handsome little feller. I think you're going to grow up to look just like your grandfather Osyka, and he was a handsome man. Take a seat on the porch, you and Dolores. I'll get us all iced tea."

Garth took a seat on the porch and before long Grandmother Osyka brought everybody a chilled glass of iced tea with a lemon wedge. Garth had never tasted iced tea before and it was a wonderful thing for him. While the threesome sipped tea a lizard scurried across the porch, sped across the lawn and disappeared into the sagebrush at the border of the lawn. On the highway below a tractor trailer shifted down to pull the grade and its engine roared fiercely.

"So sorry you lost your Adam," Grandmother Osyka said.

"It's been difficult and it's certain to get even more difficult, Mother."

"I know how it feels. When I lost your father, God bless his soul, I cried for weeks. He had been superintendent for the United Park City Mines Company for nearly twenty years, you know? He was one week away from retirement with a pension, one week. My George was killed in a cave-in in the Judge Mine over in Park City."

"I know Mother, George was my father, I was 14 at the time," Dolores said.

Grandmother Osyka thought about it for a minute, then said, "Yeah, yeah, of course he was. What a silly goose I can be."

Garth didn't remember ever having had such a supper as was served him that afternoon. Dolores pitched in and put the meal together, using food stuffs at hand. She couldn't trust Helen Osyka to help much. She was afraid the woman would get burned on the stove, or cut herself with a knife. It became evident to Dolores, from that day forward she would be doing all the cooking, and the rest of the chores, for that matter.

"Where did you get all this food, Mother?" Dolores asked.

"The Heber Mercantile delivers to me once a week. I'm not much of a cook these days, but I manage."

The threesome sat down to a tossed salad with wonderful fresh vegetables, thick slices of ham, mashed potatoes slathered in a thick gravy and huge lima beans fresh picked from the garden, all of it topped off with a rich rice pudding with cinnamon sprinklings. After eating nothing but boiled potatoes and an occasional slice of venison, the meal served to him was simply wonderful.

That night Garth was taken to his very own upstairs bedroom. He remembered it from when he visited there during Christmas. He climbed into a bed with cool, white sheets that felt marvelous to the touch. It was wonderful. He usually had several heavy, lumpy blankets piled on top of him, and the blankets were always gritty because dirt from the sod roof filtered through the cheesecloth and dropped onto his bed. He enjoyed the cool, clean sheets and he lay there and listened to his mother and grandmother talk. Their conversation drifted up the stairs and into his room, probably due to some quirk in acoustics.

"Mom, it's hard talking about this, but have you been to a doctor? You're not well."

"Heavens, no. There's nothing wrong with me. I'm healthy as a horse."

"No, there is something wrong with you; you're mind isn't what it should be."

"My heavens, daughter, how nice of you to say."

"Sorry, but you are getting older, and senility is something we need to worry about."

"So you think I'm a loony?"

"Not exactly, but let's face it, you didn't recognize Garth or me when we drove up."

"I did, too."

"No, you didn't. And you were out on the porch in your panties and bra."

"Now that is damn lie, Dolores."

Garth could hear his grandmother Osyka crying softly, and then he heard his mother crying as well. Their conversation died out for a while so he got up and looked out the window. He could see flickering neon lights at the café and gas station down on the highway The peculiar chirp of a cricket came to him from somewhere off in the night, and he watched several automobiles cruise by on the highway, probably on their way to Salt Lake. Maybe his mother would let him buy candy at the café sometime. He had only had store bought candy once in his life, a bag of Sugar Babies.

Finally his mother spoke again. "Please go get your bank statements and let me have a look."

"Dolores, dear, my bank statements are personal."

"Go get them, Mother," Dolores snapped. "I don't think you're well enough to handle your own finances."

Garth heard his grandmother shuffle off and dig through desk drawers in the room his grandfather had once used as an office when he was superintendent of the United Park City Mines Company.

There was silence for a few minutes. Finally his Mother said, "Hmm, this house is paid for and you have nearly twenty thousand dollars in Zion's First National Bank over in Heber. Mother, did you know we were over in Tabiona, practically starving . . . for years . . . you could have helped!"

"How'd I know? I'd have helped if I'd known. Besides, we weren't speaking to each other, nearly the entire time you were over in Tabiona. I told you not to marry Adam."

Dolores ignored the jibe. "You have scads of money—I can't believe it."

"Yeah, your father left me quite well fixed. I have some blue chip stocks worth about ten thousand and I have about fifty thousand in the First Security Bank in Salt Lake."

"I'd no idea . . . the money."

"Yeah, after your father died 12 years ago, the word got out that I was a rich widow. So a few men came sniffing around trying to court me, but I wouldn't give them the time a day." There was another brief silence while Dolores formulated her thoughts before she spoke. "Mother, I'll make you a deal. If you'll share this house with Garth and me, well, I'll promise to take care of you until you pass on, even if you get really sick and confused. I promise I won't dump you off in an old-age home or in a hospital. I promise to keep you right here in your home until it's your time to go."

"Do you mean it?"

"Yeah, I mean it. If I didn't mean it, I wouldn't have said it."

"Okay, it's a deal. Uh, I have been lonely every since George got killed, going on 12 years now."

"Mother."

"Yeah?"

"I'll be wanting to use some of your money to fix up this property. The money is not doing anyone any good just sitting there in those bank accounts."

"There's nothing wrong with this property."

"Starting now, you have to trust me. I promise I won't steal a penny. But I'll need money to put a new coat of paint on the house, shingle the roof, rebuild the fence, restore the lawn, clean the interior, and repair the plumbing. When I get done, the place will shine and be worth more money."

"Oh, all right. By the way, where is that husband of yours . . . Adam?"

Dolores sighed. "He died."

"No! When?"

"A few days ago. This is why we are moving in with you."

"The hell you are!" She looked Dolores over. "Who'n hell are you, anyway? How dare you barge in here?"

"I am your daughter, Dolores."

Grandmother Osyka had to think it over, but she finally said. "Yeah, yeah, of course you are. How silly of me. How long have you been here?"

"We got here today. You and I are partners now. We're in this together. I'm fixing up the property for you, remember?"

"Of course I remember. You can be so dense at times."

Dolores thought it best to move the subject along. "I want to send Garth to North School over in Heber. I enjoyed attending North School when I was a little girl."

"I'm partial to Central School, that's where I went."

"Well, Garth's going to North School."

"Have it your way."

"I've been home-schooling Garth. He's very smart and quite well-read for his age. I want him to have the best life has to offer. When he gets through high school I want to send him to Brigham Young University. I want him to be a college professor some day. It would make me so proud."

"Why not?" Grandmother Osyka asked. "He sounds like he is smart like my George. George was a mine superintendent, you know? He got his doctorate from the University of Utah in Mining Engineering . . . he was smarter than a whip."

It took Dolores two months and lots of work to make the improvements on the property. Grandmother Osyka died gently in her sleep one night and never got to enjoy the improvements, not that she really would have been aware of them. Actually, it was a blessing she died because half the time she didn't know what was going on. Dolores, being an only child, was the sole benefactor in Helen Osyka's will, and the will wasn't contested by anybody because Helen had drafted it before the dementia problems took root. Dolores got it all: the money, the property, the jewelry, the guns, the furniture, the whole shebang.

The U.S. Forest Service employee, Elroy Winterton, showed up on her step one bright fall afternoon. "I've got a powerful hankerin' for fried chicken, ma'am," were the first words out of his mouth.

Dolores laughed. "Well, you shall have it, then."

A year later Dolores married Elroy, who moved into the home there in Keetley and they had two little girls and their union was mostly loving and peaceful. But Elroy did drink quite heavily, which couldn't be denied, even though he was a good man. He was one of those happy, peaceful inebriates, never cross, never abusive, and it never interfered with his job; he continued working for the forest service.

Dolores and Garth had come full circle, they had emerged out of poverty into prosperity. Occasionally both stopped to reflect on the bad old days, but as time elapsed they brought out the old painful remembrances of Tabiona less and less. Eventually the painful memories just got buried deeply in their psyches and was left to molder.

Garth rolled through Utah's school system with ease, and he proved to be extraordinarily bright. He ended up attending MIT out in Massachusetts on a Pell Grant, a small MIT scholarship, and money from Dolores. He graduated in the top ten percentile of his graduating class and walked away with a doctorate in Aeronautical Engineering, one of the few people from Utah to attain such a goal. Shortly thereafter, a prototype of a device he began working on in the mid-1950s while working for the Pasadena Jet Propulsion Laboratory was used to build upon, and was eventually used on NASA's Mars rovers, the *Spirit*, and the *Opportunity*. The robotic arm that reached out for rocks and soil samples was, in the main, designed by Garth Folksbury from Tabiona, Utah, a barber's son.

Stretching back in time a few years from Garth's academic endeavors, to the time Dolores took her wedding vows, a new proprietor took over Folksbury's Barber Shop over in Tabiona. A shoe cobbler by the name of Harris Giinther from New Port News, Virginia, leased the tiny frame building. Harris, along with several other Easterners, had migrated into Tabiona and neighboring communities, wanting to be a part of the Western experience. When Harris disassembled the barber's sign out in front of the shop, he set a tumbleweed loose. It sat idle for a couple days until a westerly wind came by and sent it bouncing and careening out of town and out of sight.

FIXED

The first time I saw Lorraine Probst, she was sitting at a booth in Chick's Café in Heber City, Utah. That was back in 1946. She had hair as black as a stack of black cats. I think Shakespeare said something like that once. Anyway, her hair was a mass of black curls kept partially manageable with a barrette and bobby pins. It had to be the fullest, most spectacular head of hair I had ever seen. And in contrast to the coal-black hair, she wore a pure-white organza blouse with lace collar. Then there was the Hush Puppies, and plaid pedal pushers. Her skin was clear and translucent, lovely to the eye. Her breasts thrust at that blouse, trying their best to break loose of the constraints. I'm here to say that she was a looker, and what a set of blinkers. She was with her son, a three-year-old towheaded fellow. They sat eating one of Chick Café's highly acclaimed scones, slathered in butter and honey. The sight of the woman charged my batteries.

I watched them long enough that it bordered on being impolite. So I turned my attention to the menu. I decided on a hot roast beef sandwich, another Chick's specialty. After ordering, I trained my eyes back on Lorraine's hands and determined there was no wedding ring. That encouraged me. She was a beautiful sight for my war-weary eyes—I'd just recently been released from the United States Marine Corps, and served in World War II.

Keep in mind, too, that there weren't that many single ladies around Heber in those days, mostly because it was a town of only 3,000 people.

Having instantly developed an interest in the lady, I thought I'd best take a peek in the mirror behind the counter to see if I was presentable. I saw a rugged-looking fellow dressed in Western hat and Western gabardine shirt, and I knew the jeans and cowboy boots below the counter were in serviceable condition. I didn't look overly used-up, considering the toll the war had taken on me. The war had been over for a spell, yes, but I was still recovering.

I decided the sight of her called for music—trumpets or something. I yanked off my hat, plopped it on the counter and headed for the Bubbler, a Wurlitzer Juke Box. I dropped in a dime and punched up a Bing Crosby tune. He started crooning, "Have I told you lately that I love you? Have I told you once again somehow?" The melody calmed me. My nerves had been a little on edge of late. I had seen terrible things in Europe, things I needed to forget.

Apparently the song didn't set well with her because she ran across the cafe screaming like a banshee and put a Hush Puppy through the front of the Bubbler, smashing the 78 RPM record all to shit. Then she grabbed her son and hustled out the front door, leaving the scones uneaten and an unfiltered Camel cigarette smoldering in the ashtray. When she got to her car, a '46 Ford Flathead convertible, black with red interior, she kicked the front passenger door for good measure and tossed her son into the front seat. The top had been lowered because it was summertime. She circled around the front of the car with her arms outstretched like the wings of an airplane, screaming all the time like a son of a bitch.

The owner of the café came out from the kitchen and surveyed the damage to the Wurlitzer. "Well, I'll be a sad, sorry bastard," he said.

"What's wrong with her?" I asked.

"Lorraine lost her husband on Omaha Beach during the allied invasion of Normandy and she's been a little screwy ever since."

"What'll it cost to have that juke box repaired?"

"At least two hundred dollars."

"She drives a fancy car. Does she have money?"

"No, but her daddy does. She lives up there at the head of Daniel's Canyon in that giant California Mission house. Big Ned Probst enjoys telling me about his house, pert-near ever time I see him. He's mighty proud of it. She moved back in with her parents after her husband was killed."

"Is Probst the fellow owns the big sheep outfit up at the head of Daniel's Canyon?"

"Yup. I'll just bill ol' man Probst for the damages. It's not the first time she's came in here and broken shit."

I walked out to talk to Lorraine. She was still sitting in her car, slumped over the steering wheel, sobbing.

My light-blue '45 Studebaker pickup was parked in front of her. Being she was extremely agitated, I hoped she wouldn't run into it when she drove away.

"The owner said he'll just bill your daddy for the damages," I said, by way of starting a conversation.

She looked up and seemed surprised that I'd take the time to relay such a message. From close in she was even more beautiful, and her perfume—mild and understated—was drawing me in like a moth to the flame.

"What're you bumpin' your gums about?"

"The owner in there says your daddy will pay for the Wurlitzer."

"As always. Who are you?" she asked.

"David Crittenden. I just mustered out of the Marines."

"Who gives a shit? I don't want to hear anything more about military shit."

"What set you off in there?"

"That Bing Crosby song was our song, Jake Barns and mine. Jake was my husband; he was killed on Omaha Beach. The orchestra was playing that song when we met."

"Sorry he had to die."

"Don't be. It wasn't your fault. That stinkin' war took him from me. Sometimes I just go screwy when I'm reminded of that."

"Mommy, I'm hungry," the little boy said, jumping up and down on the seat. "I want my scone."

"No, not today, Billy, we're going home."

"Aw, Ma . . ."

"Sit down, we're leaving," Lorraine said.

He jumped a couple more times just for spite and then he flopped down in the seat, crossed his arms over his little chest and started pouting.

"Hey, Joe College, come'n see me," she said, winking and driving away.

Was it so obvious I'd gone to college? I stood there watching her leave. No doubt about it, the woman had just flirted with me. I knew instinctively that getting involved with a doll like her was just plain stupid. Regardless, I watched her until she was out of sight, and then made up my mind to get involved, no matter the consequences. In fact, I decided I was going up there the next day to look at the scenery, and see her. I was lonely. The last woman I'd been with was a French whore, and that saying about a French whore's heart is right on the money.

I was born and raised in Coalville, Utah, and my parents died while I was fighting in Europe. I can scarcely think about it without tearing up. Anyway, after I returned from the war, I settled the estate affairs in Coalville and moved to Heber to take a low-paying clerking job at the Heber Mercantile. Mom and Dad owed everybody in sight, so when the estate was tallied up, there was none left over for me. If Lorraine had crashed into my Studebaker. I wouldn't have had the money to fix it.

The job at the Heber Mercantile was a stopgap position. My long-range plan was to teach history at Wasatch High School. I wanted to be a Wasatch Wasp. Before I went off to war I'd earned an MA in history from the University of Utah. I wanted to put that advanced degree to work.

I drove up Daniel's Canyon the next morning, edged my Studebaker through a big gate with an arch that said, "The Lucky Deuce." A mansion stood there at the end of the drive, butting up against a grove of Douglas Fir. It was the biggest house I'd ever seen. The yard was meticulously landscaped. Several groundskeepers were puttering around, trimming hedges and mowing a lawn the size of a football field. As I drove up to the entrance I smelled freshly mowed grass, and sheep shit.

Lorraine met me at the door and invited me into a large, sprawling, living room. The floors were made of ten-inch-wide planking stained light brown; a portion of the walls were stacked stone and there was a cathedral ceiling. The walls had trophy big-game heads, and there were bookshelves loaded with expensive volumes of leather-bound books. The room had a masculine feel to it and the furnishings were expensive and solid. I particularly liked a brown Sonoma leather chair and ottoman set. I couldn't see the rest of the house, but I imagined it to be as sumptuous as the living room.

She ran her blinkers over me with studied thoroughness and I suppose she liked what she saw because she gave me a knowing little smile, a smile that said she had taken my measure, that we were an item. It's kind of sad, and thrilling at the same time to be such an easy conquest, but her beauty had turned me into putty.

Thus our relationship began without the slightest observance to custom. It didn't require dating, candlelight dinners, and meeting the folks, or my having to fumble around to cop that first feel, or that first kiss. Not by a long shot, the romance just simply sparked into life spontaneously.

"Wait here, Joe College," she said, winking. She went into the kitchen and I overheard her asking a woman I presumed to be her mother if she'd baby-sit the little boy. Lorraine explained to the woman that she was going horseback riding with a handsome fellow named David Crittenden.

"You never listen to my advice," her mother said, "but I'll give it to you anyway. I don't think that's a good idea, your Jake hasn't been dead long enough for you to go gallivanting around with another fellow."

"I can't spend the rest of my life grieving over Jake. I won't."

"What'll people think?"

"Who gives a shit?"

"Your father will not be pleased."

"Who gives a shit?"

"What about your, uh, your fragile mental condition? Will the fellow be tolerant of that?"

"I can't say, but I'd hope so."

"Don't you think you should see that psychiatrist in Provo a few more times before you start dating?"

"To hell with him and all the rest of 'em. I like the looks of this David Crittenden. He is tall, blond, rugged, manly, and it looks like he can hold his own in a scrap, if another man tries to cut in."

"You'd like that, wouldn't you?"

"Men fighting over me is never dull."

There was a silence for a few moments. "You're makin' a mistake," her mother finally said, and then I heard silverware clinking.

"Could be, but I don't care," Lorraine answered.

I don't know whether Lorraine intended for me to overhear the conversation. But since I had, I knew I should bolt from the Lucky Deuce, an empire built on sheep, but I couldn't bring myself to do it.

Lorraine stepped back into the living room. "Can you ride a horse, Joe College?" she asked, transfixing me with those gorgeous blinkers.

"Listen, doll, I was saddle-bronc riding champion at the Oakley, Utah, rodeo just before the war. I think that was back in 'thirty-nine."

"So you like bragging?"

"Well, you asked me if I can ride. I can, quite well. I was raised on a small cattle ranch up in Coalville, Utah—all that's gone now, though. Both my parents died when I was over in Europe."

"Well, since you can ride, let's take a ride up the Row Bench Trail until we top out on the summit and then we can sit and look down into the Strawberry Valley. We'll take a picnic lunch."

"Okay."

"We should be able to see mule deer and some of father's sheep, not that that'll be much of a thrill—the sheep, I mean. But the wooly critters do produce a lot of money, as you can see." She swept her hand around, referencing the Lucky Deuce.

"We haven't left yet? Yippee-yi-yo-ki-yay."

"You cowboys," she said. "It seems to me you've been bucked off on your head too many times." She gave me a 24-carat smile that made me tingle all the way to my toes. There is nothing quite like a beautiful woman's smile. "Sit tight for about ten minutes and I'll pack us a picnic lunch. Do you like fried chicken and potato salad?"

"Yeah."

"Okay, sit tight."

"Shake a leg, I'm dead set on this scheme," I said.

I spent ten minutes reading from a leather-bound volume of short stories written by O'Henry when Big Ned came in and interrupted.

"And you are?" he asked, standing there glaring at me. He must have suspected I was there to call on his daughter.

Big Ned looked like a candidate for a stroke. He was wheezy, and had a roll of belly fat hanging over his belt buckle; he was flushed and sweating. I would have bet anything he had high blood pressure and a bad heart. He looked to be about sixty and he had thick, gray hair that started at the top of his head and probably went all the way to his toes. I could see he had a mat of gray hair on his chest that looked like a Brillo pad.

"David Crittenden."

"What are you doing here?"

"Sparking your daughter."

"The hell you are."

"Yeah, we're about to go on a picnic."

"Do you know she is mentally . . . unstable?"

"Yeah."

"So what do you want with her? Aren't there plenty of normal gals you can spark?"

"She's beautiful. I want to spark her."

"You're not aiming to get into her drawers are you? She has problems enough without that happening and complicating her life."

"Why, sir, you surprise me. Of course not," I said, lying through my teeth.

Of course I was going to try to get into her drawers. After all, I'm a male *homo sapien*, hardwired for it. But now that I'm older I regret having that earlier weakness of the flesh, even if it was mainly brought on by Mother Nature. And my reaction to Big Ned was off-base, he was only a caring father protecting his daughter. I'm more mature these days and not so impetuous and selfish, nor am I still a horn dog like I was when I was young.

Winston Churchill said he did his best work later in life after his libido quieted . . . I share those sentiments.

"See that you don't," he said. "We're docking sheep right now and we could easily include you in one of the procedures."

"I wouldn't part with my nuts without putting up one hell of a squall—I've grown quite fond of them."

He laughed, but quickly cut it short. Then he just stood there glaring at me, so I glared back. Finally, he decided nothing was being gained by the glaring contest, so he walked off to another part of the house. So, there it was, I had met Big Ned.

Lorraine and I saddled a pair of fine horses and started off toward the very top of Daniel's Canyon, up into nosebleed country. The Aspens along the trail rustled in a gentle breeze and occasionally there were groups of Lodgepole pines or Douglas fir swaying from the wind. Everything was a treat to the eye, smelled good, and seemed freshly scrubbed by a recent rain.

"Hey, Joe College, let me know if you see a stand of Lodgepole about six inches in diameter," Lorraine said.

"Why do you call me Joe College?" I asked.

"You went to college didn't you? I can tell by the way you act."

"Yeah, but . . ."

"Well, there you go."

"Why do I need to keep a lookout for six-inch Lodgepole?"

"Big Ned is building another horse corral on the Lucky Deuce."

"Ever expanding, eh?"

"That's Big Ned, my daddy."

We topped out on the summit. It seemed like we were sitting right on the upper extremity of the world. I thought I could feel the presence of God. The Strawberry Valley stretched before us as far as the eye could see. The landscape consisted of varied shades of green represented by sagebrush, Aspens, Spruce, Douglas fir, Quaking Aspen, and Lodgepole pine—not to mention the multicolored lilies, grasses, and sedges in the upland meadows. Then way off in the background was Strawberry Reservoir, twinkling silver and blue in the noontime sun. The panorama gladdened the heart and I doubt that the most capable landscape artist could have painted it and brought it to life, putting to use the mostly synthetic-generated colors of the artist's palette.

Lorraine and I sat on a big Douglas fir that had been downed by the wind. After looking over the breathtaking valley I swept my eyes over her and found her as lovely as the panorama stretching before us. I kissed her and she gave no resistance. I had been right in regards to the tacit love affair that had spontaneously sparked between us just yesterday.

After the kiss, she walked over to her roan mare that was tied off to an Aspen tree and pulled a blanket from a saddlebag. She spread the blanket on meadow grass sprinkled with wild asters, Beardtongue, and bluebells. Then she disrobed with an economy of motion and stood watching me and waiting. She just posed before me with no hint of self-consciousness about being in the altogether. Her body was a work of art. I'm here to say that she had a set of pins that were to die for, and a set of breasts that inspired poetry, even if I wasn't much of a rhymester.

"Well, shake a leg, Joe College," she said.

My mother didn't raise a fool, so I pulled off my clothes and joined her on the blanket. I can't remember ever having a union with a woman that gave me more pleasure. I suppose it was the whole package that did it for me. It had to be the natural setting, the gentle breeze, the smell of the forest, and the sight of her nakedness and her seeming vulnerability—the whole package. I had an orgasm so powerful that it wracked my entire body in waves of indescribable pleasure.

After we finished and got dressed, she said, "Now you're going to have to marry me or I'll tell my daddy what happened here. When he finds out about you puttin' your little thingy in me, he'll dock you like his buck sheep."

"Marry you?"

"That's right, Jake was killed in that horrible war and I'm givin' you permission to take his place."

"What about love?"

"What about it? It's overrated. This'll teach you to make whoopee on a first date."

"What about at least getting to know each other?"

"After what just happened, I think we know each other quite well."

"Marry you?"

"That's right, if you value your testicles."

Two months later I married Lorraine Probst and I moved into that stately log house on the Lucky Deuce. Her father, Big Ned, hired me on as a sheep man. I was happy to be able to quit clerking at the Heber Mercantile. In hiring me as a sheep man, Big Ned promised to teach me the sheep business from top to bottom and then promote me to foreman.

He explained it this way: "I don't much like you—there's just something about you that pisses me off—but I do want my daughter cared for in the manner she has grown accustomed."

"Thank you, sir, for being forthright," I managed to say. "I don't like you much, either."

All through this impetuous romance and marriage I never gave Lorraine's mental disorder a second thought. So what if she was screwy? Being slightly screwy myself, thanks to my war experience, I'd developed a devil-may-care attitude. In plain language, I didn't much give a shit what happened to me.

Seven months after we married she gave birth to our baby boy that we named Josh. Apparently she conceived during that first wonderful union at the summit of Daniel's Canyon. We were, I thought, deliriously happy during those first few months of marriage, in fact, I officially adopted Billy Jake, Jr., and that was a happy occasion. His new handle became Billy Crittenden.

The problems didn't begin until after the birth.

We left the Heber Hospital with our new son and we were giddy, and talking, and listening to the radio. A deep voice on the radio tells us in a toothpaste commercial that "You can compare the action of Kolynos Toothpaste to the action of a jeweler's polish." Then just as we were rolling up the driveway at the Lucky Deuce, Bing Crosby came on and started in with, "Have I Told You Lately That I Love You."

I shut off the radio immediately, just as a precaution. But it was too late; she began screaming like a banshee and wouldn't let up. I pulled the car up in front of the house and tried to take the baby from her, but she wouldn't hear of it. So I helped her into the house, wanting to do something useful. She stepped up to the couch and threw the baby down like a sack of potatoes and collapsed into an easy chair with her legs folded up under her. Then she started in with the rocking back and forth . . . and the whimpering shit went on for months.

Not once after that did she so much as acknowledge our newborn. It was as if she had cut all ties with him, and with me, and with her parents, too, for that matter. It hurt us all. It hurt me in particular I think because I needed the love and attention like she'd given me when we were first married—I craved it. But we had all been summarily dismissed from her life. Big Ned and I finally figured we had to get help and we hired a nanny to care for the children. Then we started looking around for professional help.

Lorraine spent her days rocking back and forth and whimpering, and her nights sleeping coiled up in a fetal position, as if she were trying to insulate herself from the predations of a hostile world.

This rocking back and forth and whimpering went on for another year until I happened on a possible way to fix her mental condition. I learned that the famed psychiatrist, Walter Freeman, was going to be at the LDS Hospital in Salt Lake beginning September 14, 1947. He had pioneered the prefrontal lobotomy for people with irremediable mental disorders, this back in 1935. Freeman set up a clinic at a future date to examine the seriously mentally ill. He had been going from state to state offering his services to those in need.

A prefrontal lobotomy is a brain operation wherein the surgeon drills holes in the patient's forehead and goes in with a long, slender medical instrument and simply scrambles the frontal lobe. Usually after the operation the patient was better able to cope with the rigors of everyday living, but they also usually came away from the operation docile, incontinent, and detached.

Rosemary Kennedy, John F. Kennedy's sister, was lobotomized. Her father, Joseph Kennedy, agreed to have it done because she was willful and too interested in boys ... not to mention she was a little screwy. Rosemary was twenty-three at the time. She was incapacitated after the operation; it rendered her childlike, nearly non-verbal, and incontinent. She spent the remainder of her life at St. Coletta's Institute for Backward Children in Jefferson, Wisconsin.

The American Medical Association met as a panel in 1941 and concluded that the prefrontal lobotomy should only be considered an experiment. It was never sanctioned as a viable operation to cure mental disorders.

But that didn't stop Walter Freeman from performing 3,429 of the barbaric procedures.

I was willing to risk the possibility of changing her, simply to recover her as my wife and to restore her as the mother of our children. With that in mind, Lorraine, Big Ned, and I drove to Salt Lake to see if we could get her fixed.

Big Ned and I dragged Lorraine in to see Walter Freeman. During that meeting we formed a consensus that we should come back the next day and have the operation. For Freeman it wasn't a hard decision, he stood to make two grand scrambling Lorraine's frontal lobe. All during the examination Lorraine never uttered a word. She just sat in a chair with her legs tucked up under her and rocked.

After the examination, I asked Big Ned to take her back to the car because I wanted a word in private with Freeman. "So what's wrong with her doc?"

He looked straight at me, unwavering, cleared his throat, and said, "People who qualify for the prefrontal lobotomy usually suffer from anxiety, depression, obsessive-compulsive disorder, mental retardation, schizophrenia, or one or more of any number of disorders. There are around three hundred forms of mental illness we know about and have documented. In my opinion, Lorraine has a form of schizophrenia. This was more than likely precipitated by the loss of her husband in the war. She's unlikely to get better unless we do this operation."

"Okay," I said, "let's do it." After that he walked me through the operating room. There were five side-by-side beds. I expected elaborate medical equipment: devices for emergencies, stethoscopes, blood pressure cuffs, but the room was bare except for the beds.

"What else do you want to know, Mr."—he looked on his chart—"Mr. Crittenden?"

"What is this refinement you refer to, the one that speeds up the time it takes to perform a prefrontal lobotomy?"

"Simply put, instead of drilling holes in the forehead to access the frontal lobe, I go in just above the eyes, with an ice pick through the tear ducts. Once I access the tear duct, I use a hammer to pound the ice pick through the exterior membrane of the brain, and then I waggle the ice pick back and forth like a windshield wiper and destroy the frontal lobe. Once I destroy the connection with the thalamus, the patient should be cured of the mental disorder."

"Good God, an ice pick?"

"Afraid so. Sounds bad, but I assure you the operation is relatively painless and highly effective."

"And you really do think the operation will work for Lorraine?"

"I have performed thousands of these operations and the success ratio has been most satisfactory."

"We'll be here at ten a.m. tomorrow."

"All right, the operation costs two thousand dollars. How will you pay? Cash or check?"

"Cash," I said, confident that Big Ned would pony up the money.

"All right then, see you tomorrow."

Lorraine survived the barbaric operation and it gave her two years without the rocking back and forth and the whimpering, but that hardly mattered because she was no longer Lorraine. The operation took away her personality and turned her into a docile, robot-like creature that never smiled, cried, shouted, cooed, laughed, teased, or did anything that might identify her as human. She pissed herself and forgot how to eat. She forgot nearly everything. In fact, she lost so many skills and functions that it took me nearly a year to retrain her, just so she could function on a minimal basis.

After those two years passed, she died of a cerebral hemorrhage. It was sad, yeah, but I tried to look at it philosophically. I had to, it was the only way I could cope. But I believed Lorraine was doomed from the moment she lost her first husband on the beach at Normandy—that it just took her a while to actually die.

It was very sad, but all wasn't lost, because I survived the robotic days and her eventual death, even though at the bitter end I cried days on end, and that's not easy for a cowboy to admit, most of us consider ourselves as tough as boiled owl shit. Our little boys survived it as well, and, hey, life goes on.

When the AMA put a stop to prefrontal lobotomies as experiments, it came too late, thousands of people, including my lovely Lorraine, had already been mutilated and turned into vegetables. I would have rather had the whimpering, crying, and rocking back, because those last two years were hell on earth.

After the AMA put a stop to the prefrontal lobotomy, Walter Freeman became inconsolable. He never stopped defending the operation and he spent the last twenty years of his life driving around the country visiting the people he had lobotomized, hoping to find them in peachy mental health. He went searching for his legacy.

Big Ned built me and the boys a new home on his property at the top of Daniel's Canyon right after the lobotomy. He wanted a safe place for Lorraine and her sons, and it was safe, but Lorraine still died. Lorraine had been dead nearly three years when Walter Freeman popped in one day, knocked on the door of our new home and asked, "How is Lorraine doing?" while consulting a chart he was carrying, to make sure he had the name right.

"You killed her, you bastard," I said.

"How so?" he asked.

"In the beginning, the operation killed her personality, who she was, and in the end it killed her as a being; she had a cerebral hemorrhage. You are a fraud, a prick."

"Young man, surely you are mistaken. The prefrontal lobotomy was a godsend for those people here in America that had severe mental disorders. Quite frankly, I am proud to have pioneered the operation here in America."

"Climb down off my porch, get into your car, and drive away before I take a notion to kick the living shit out of you."

He left and not long after that, he died. He never found the legacy he was looking for. The prefrontal lobotomy had been a bust. His life's work hadn't lived up to expectations.

I am the foreman here at the Lucky Deuce sheep ranch and I'm busy raising my two boys. Never a day goes by that I don't think about Lorraine, which brings an ache to my heart. I had, in the final analysis, loved her with all my being. The indifference and angst I brought back from the war disappeared and now I very much cared about my well-being. I have a sheep operation to ramrod and two little boys that I am hoping will develop into successful and happy grownups.

And here's the kicker, Big Ned and I have become good friends. He comes over to the house and we talk about sheep and drink giggle water; we pour a couple snifters of Maker's Mark bourbon whiskey and bump our gums. He misses Lorraine, and God knows, so do I.

REDRESS

Some forty years ago, Dan Walton, a high school chum of mine, talked me into attending Dixie Junior College in St. George, Utah. We had just graduated from dear old Wasatch High School in Heber City, Utah; we'd been Wasatch Wasps. If I hadn't listened to him and gone about my business as a low-skilled laborer of some sort, I probably wouldn't have brought myself such shame.

This shame and torment began back in 1962, the era of the Hula-Hoop, fin cars, Elvis, and the Beatles—we're talking a long time ago. I resisted Dan's urgings for most of the summer following our high school graduation, but I finally gave in. He gleefully made all the preparations for us, by setting up housing in the men's dormitories, landing jobs at the student cafeteria, and arranging enrollment. Out of guilt, I helped him with the enrollment part by providing my high school transcript and a couple bits of other relevant information . . . hey, I felt obligated to contribute just a little.

My grade point average at Wasatch was a 2.0, a lousy C average. And I suspect that I'd been given an administrative pass—or the GPA wouldn't have been that high—probably so the teachers wouldn't have to deal with me further.

Regardless, Dixie College still accepted me, Clay Cummings, poor grades and all. I guess my tuition money spent as well as the next guy's. So, I was headed off to college and I didn't have the slightest idea how to study or survive at an institution of higher learning. I was truly scared. During high school, from the ninth through the 12th grade, I'd never carried a book home to study, not once. I was as much suited to attend college as Audie Murphy was suited to play Nose Guard in the NFL.

I suspect Dan wanted me as a college roommate because I had a bitchin' '55 Ford Country Sedan for chasing the ladies. Incidentally, the only reason I can put down this narrative these many years later is because I eventually straightened up and got a good education, I became a journalist, but I didn't stick with that very long either, but I did retain the accumulated knowledge. If I'd had to put down this narrative at the time these misadventures happened, I would have been hard put to do it.

The Ford was chopped, shaved, nosed, decked, and painted Twilight Mist lavender. It was a low-rider with Lake Plugs, Appleton Spotlights, tuck 'n' roll Naughahyde interior, chrome tailpipe extensions, fiesta-style spinner hubcaps, dice hung off the rearview mirror, and it had an eight ball for a gearshift knob. I'd named her, "The Drifter."

During that era it was a highly prized auto. It had such appeal that whenever I picked up women, they'd immediately begin pulling off their clothes. Not really. Actually at that time in my life I was still a virgin, a fact that I assiduously hid from my friends. And back then, as now, it was jokingly said that the only virgins were fat, ugly fourth-graders.

After driving 300 miles south to St. George, we pulled up in front of the administration building to check in. I was scared. It was all I could do to get out of the car and walk into the place. I considered myself a fraud and out of place on a college campus. I thought the administrators would see through my charade and laugh at me and tell me to go home and take up a career more befitting my aptitude, a career involving picks and shovels, or masonry hods. But I finally mustered enough courage and walked in.

The lady who took our money and checked us in was nice. We paid tuition, dormitory fees, parking fees, and I ended up shelling out twenty-five dollars for a biology 101 lab fee. The woman behind the counter had rosacea. Her face was beet red and she must have been eighty years old and fatter than a Guernsey cow, but she was pleasant, and pleasant was what I needed about then because I was ready to cut and run.

Back outside, a pickup was parallel parked just in front of my Ford. It said "Scallion Construction Company" on the door. Two young men climbed out of the truck and approached. A beefy guy all in denims with a yellow hard hat walked up to me and got in my face. He had removed the sleeves from his shirt to show off a hefty set of biceps. These days, during the early twenty-first century, it would be said that he was "shredded." Shredded or not, the jackass was invading my space and I didn't like it.

"Another college ass wipe," he said, sneering at me.

"Not yet," I said, "but starting tomorrow."

"St. George is overrun with you punks."

"Smile when you say that, stranger," I said, remembering *The Virginian*.

"What'n hell does that mean?" the guy asked.

"Come on, Clay, let's boogie," Dan said, standing there behind me and looking ashen.

"Climb it, Tarzan," I said, shooting him the bird. I don't know why I did that. I wasn't a fighter. I was only 5' 11" and 150 pounds, and capable of bench pressing about one hundred pounds on a good day.

"Far out. You dare to shoot me the bird. You must be suicidal. Do you know who I am? My daddy owns Scallion Construction Company, the largest construction company in southern Utah. Not only do I come from power, but I can beat the shit out of just about any man that walks. Right now, my daddy's company is renovating the Latter-Day-Saints temple," he said, proudly.

"Who gives a shit? Why are you in my face?"

"You pulled in front of me and almost ran me off the road back up there by the turnoff to Hurricane with that lead-sled you call a car."

"Hey, man, I didn't mean to pull in front of you. Sorry."

"Sorry doesn't cut it," he said, turning to his friend and laughing.

That emboldened his friend, who was a look-alike for Ernest Borgnine, and who also took a key to the side of my car. I stood watching in horror and the beefy one in the sleeveless shirt sucker-punched me. I just remember the ground coming up to meet me and then nothing.

I came too a few minutes later because Dan poured cold water on my face. He'd gotten the water from a water fountain inside the admin building.

The piece of shit with the key had done more damage to the side of my car while I was out. When I came to I was more concerned about my car than my face—it bothered me so greatly, in fact, that I felt sick to my stomach. The paint job on my car consisted of ten coats of lacquer and it was buffed out to a mirror finish. It was twilight mist lavener. The paint job had cost me $500, and that was a lot of dough back in 1962. And to think that piece of shit had called it a lead-sled. In the olden days, holes used to be filled with lead, rather than Bondo.

I did my best trying to forget the damage to the Drifter and managed to drive Dan and I across campus to check in at the men's dormitory. It was a new building situated on the outskirts of St. George. We reported to the dorm supervisor, a fellow named Rudy Carpenter, who was living there in one of the apartments with his wife and two kids. He told his wife he would only be a minute and then he escorted us to our apartment.

It was blistering hot that long-ago September. The thermometer was hovering around 100° Fahrenheit. St. George is located about a hundred miles north of Las Vegas and it shares much of the same blast furnace-like weather. The dorm was a two-story affair and we were to live on the second story. While we were climbing a set of exterior steps, Rudy, who was leading, suddenly yelped and lunged backward, nearly knocking Dan and me down the steps. Some wise ass had coiled a dead rattlesnake on the steps. But once we realized the snake was dead, we laughed.

"Boys will be boys," Rudy said.

After we came up onto a long cement porch, I stopped at the railing and took a moment to look over the campus. The Utah state legislature had recently appropriated money for new buildings and improvements; it was apparent that the men's dorm wasn't the only new building. The cafeteria was new, and so were the science building, heating plant, and gymnasium. And there were lots of landscaping projects in progress. They don't call Utah the beehive state for nothing. For the first time, I felt kind of happy about being there.

I turned to Rudy. "Hey, man, where do you suppose the wise ass found the rattler?"

"Don't call me 'man'; my name's Rudy. Rattlers? Are you kiddin'? Look around most anywhere out there." He swept his hand across the desert landscape.

It was true; the snake could have come from most anywhere out there. The dorm and parking lot were carved out of a large expanse of sagebrush. "Are there lots of rattlers around here?" I asked, shuddering.

Rudy grinned. "We have our fair share; this is the country for them."

Our room was . . . all right. It had cinderblock walls but the appointments were Spartan. I'd seen worse. I spent a year in a reform school in Murray, Utah, a SLC suburb. The room was worse there, way worse. That happened when I was fifteen. I stole the neighbor's car and ran it into a sign post at the end of an island on Heber's main street, a screw up I never repeated.

It created a hell of a scandal in Heber. At the time, my mom was a homemaker and my father operated a small newspaper in Heber. Both were devout members of the LDS church and from that time forward they stopped speaking to me, except for just a few everyday routine things that simply had to be said. Not surprisingly, my self-respect went directly into the toilet. Mom and Dad have passed on, but they maintained the cloak of silence, pretty much, to their dying days. I wish they could have seen that stealing that car was a one-time thing and that, in the end, I turned out being a pretty good guy.

But I was talking about the dorm room there at Dixie. One good thing about that room, it was brand new. We were the first students to live there.

"If you boys get to drinking and tearing shit up, I'll throw you out with no refund on your money. Is that plain enough?" Rudy asked.

"That's plain enough, man," Dan said.

"Don't call me man. Another thing that'll get you kicked out on your ass: Do not bring girls into your rooms. Never. I'm not running a whorehouse here. There's a list of the dorm rules down in the laundry room. You be sure to read them and adjust your behavior accordingly."

I decided I liked Rudy. He spoke his mind.

When we got our gear stowed away, I stepped out of our room to walk around and meet some of the Dixie Junior College student body. Some fellow was riding up and down the sidewalk on a skateboard, a Roller Derby Board. Skateboarding was a new thing back then and I'd been checking out the different brands, thinking about buying one. I walked down to talk to the guy. He looked interesting, even if he did have long hair and was sort of scroungy-looking.

"Hey man, my name's Clay Cummings," I said.

"Howdy, man. My friends call me Scrotum," he said, thrusting off on the board and zipping down the walk only to hit a wide crack in the sidewalk and crash. The crash was a bad one. He twisted his ankle and was in excruciating pain.

"Hop to my car and I'll take you to the hospital," I said, pointing to the Ford.

He hopped on one foot and climbed into the front seat and was writhing around in pain, but he managed to say, "Bitchin' car, but what happened to the side?"

About that time I got a whiff of body odor. It was an old odor, apparently layered and magnified to a high intensity. I took the time to roll down all the windows. I would have had to anyway due to the heat.

"Some construction worker I never heard of keyed it today. Then his buddy sucker-punched me." I didn't need pointing out where I'd been punched, I had a huge mouse over my right eye and the eye itself was threatening to close shut.

"Bummer. There's just no accounting for some people's manners."

His ankle had ballooned to twice its normal size and obviously hurt like the devil. His face was white with green tinges around the edges.

Doctor Bart Anderson examined him at the Dixie Regional Medical Center, wrote him a prescription for painkillers, and sent him home with a set of crutches.

When we got to the dorm—Scrotum lived there, too, it turned out— Dan was standing on the sidewalk out front, looking hacked off. "Where'n hell have you been?"

"I had to take Scrotum to the doctor; he twisted his ankle."

"Scrotum? Is that really your name?" He smiled widely, looking at my new friend.

"Yeah, man, that's his nickname," I said, shrugging my shoulders, and scrunching up my lips as I walked by him.

As we walked away, Scrotum looked back over his shoulder and explained how he got the nickname. I don't know why he bothered because he didn't owe Dan an explanation. I guess he was just proud of the nickname and wanted to talk about it. "When I was a kid I swam in my Dad's pool every day and I always stayed in so long that I got wrinkled. So Dad took to calling me Scrotum and it has sort of stuck."

"Far out," I said. Dan and I laughed over that, and then I took Scrotum's arm and helped him to his room. I was happy to find out it was on the first floor. Getting him up a flight of stairs wouldn't have been fun, and he refused using the crutches. He was too macho, I guess.

His room was austere, to say the least. His closet contained only one pair of jeans neatly arranged on a hanger, a T-shirt neatly arranged on another, and a pair of sandals neatly arranged on the floor. He wore an identical outfit. I suppose the outfit in the closet was part of a rotation system.

After looking over his closet I looked into his chest of drawers which was open and unmissable and I could see one pair of white socks and one pair of men's underwear, folded neatly. I presumed he was wearing identical socks and underwear. Next, I took a peek in his bathroom and discovered that he had a comb, toothbrush, toothpaste, hand soap, and shampoo. That's it. I don't know how he survived with so few things.

Scrotum watched me snoop about, smiling the whole time. Once I was done with the snooping, I shrugged my shoulders and looked over at him. "Solid threads," I said, sarcastically.

"Ha! You've got that right," he said, laughing. "I'm your basic minimalist," he said.

"Well, out of sight," I said, "good for you."

"Yeah, out of sight."

"So, where are you from?"

"I'm from Vegas. My ol' man lives down there and he is richer than God."

"Is God rich?"

He looked surprised by that question. "I thought he was."

"I think he's considered rich in a spiritual sense, but I don't think he has worldly riches."

"All right, have it your way, man. He has big houses, big cars, big rings, big bank accounts, big swimming pools, big gold necklaces, and big-tit girlfriends. He might not be as rich as God, but he's got some serious coin."

"Are you going to take me to Vegas?" I want to see all this stuff."

"Sure, but you won't like it. Mom's dead and Dad's a dick."

I laughed. "We'll just stay away from your old man while we're there."

"Hey, dude, come to my party tonight. I'll have all the wine you can drink. It should be worth a few grins."

"What about Rudy and the no-alcohol rule?"

"Hose Rudy."

"Right! What time?"

"Seven bells."

"Okay, I'll show up. Can I bring my roommate, Dan?"

"Does he have leprosy?"

"No."

"Okay then, man, bring him."

I laughed and turned to leave.

"Thanks for the ride to the hospital," he said.

"No problem . . . uh, I'm just curious, do you own a car?"

He looked at me like I was stupid. "I'm a minimalist."

"Right."

There were ten or so guys at the wine party; all were dorm residents. Scrotum had three gallons of Mogen David cooling in an old wash tub filled with chipped ice. The party looked like it was going to be a lot of fun and I saw there were plenty of Dixie Junior College students to meet. I thought it was a great way to kick off the beginning of the quarter.

Scrotum was already slobbering drunk and babbling. "No party is complete without a wino," he said, slurring his words badly.

"Huh?" I asked.

"Huh?" Dan asked.

"What do you mean?" a student named Hank asked.

"Don't be such retards," Scrotum said, looking around at all of us. "Fer crisesakes, Clay, cruise downtown in your Ford and pick up a wino and bring him back to the party. We need to share this wine with a wino, it's only fitting. I'm quite sure winos like wine, right?" he asked with a twinkle in his eye.

I decided to humor him, so I headed for the Ford. As I left I saw several bags of fast food, crackers, cheeses, chips, and cans full of mixed nuts, all sitting on his cinder block window ledge. I grabbed a handful of nuts on the way out. It was obvious that Scrotum had a larger budget than your typical college student, even if he didn't flaunt it.

"What if Rudy catches us at this?" I asked.

"To hell with ol' Rudy," Scrotum said.

Dan and I found a wino leaning up against a building down on St. George Boulevard. We loaded him in the Ford and wheeled him back to the party. He was dressed in tatters and it didn't look like he had bathed in months; he smelled of campfires, musty clothing, urine, cigarettes, and he reeked of alcohol.

When he saw the jugs of wine cooling in that wash tub, he thought he'd died and gone to heaven.

"Get a Dixie Cup and help yourself. My name is Scrotum," our host said.

"I'm Jake," the wino said. "Mogen David is one of my favorite wines." He thought about that for a moment and added, "Hell, actually, any type of wine can be my favorite."

We were all blitzed and that seemed to be just about the funniest thing any of us had ever heard. We all laughed until one student blew Mogen David through his nose, which ramped up the laughter even more.

The party was, I suppose, your typical student gathering involving alcohol: laughter, chatter, arguments, and a fist fight. A pair of students beat each other senseless over some girl they had both been dating. Scrotum ran them off. "Pieces of shit," he said.

After I'd lapped up more wine than is healthy, I sat down on a window sill and got thinking about the day's events. I couldn't believe how much had happened in a single day. Earlier that morning, that seemed ages ago, we had still been on the highway driving toward St. George. Then I'd enrolled in college, gotten punched in the face, seen a dead rattler, met Scrotum, and gotten drunk on Mogen David wine. At that time I should have staggered off to bed. But no, I was drunk and feeling no pain so I concocted a scheme to get even with the construction worker who'd punched me in the face.

I met Scrotum in the hallway. I'd been using his head. "Do you want to take a cruise in the Ford?" I would have asked Dan, but Dan was too uptight to get involved in what I had in mind.

"I'm having a party here, man," he said, limping around while he talked. "I'm trying my best to see that everybody gets knee-crawling drunk."

"Everybody is knee crawling drunk; they won't even miss you."

"So, man, where do you want to go?"

"I want to get even with the bastard that punched me in the face."

"By doing what? I'm not interested in going to the slammer just so Clay Cummings can get his jollies."

"I don't know exactly what I want to do to get revenge. I thought I'd ride over to the LDS Temple and look over Scallion Construction Company's equipment. The big ape that punched me said that his father's company is remodeling the LDS Temple."

"Why would you want to look over their equipment?"

"I was thinking that I might find a piece of heavy equipment and pour sugar in the gas tank, or something like that. It's childish of me, but it would make me feel better damaging his father's equipment. It would be insane to go after the big ape himself. You should have seen the guy. He was built like a brick shithouse."

"I don't know, man, I'm a peace-loving guy."

"It sounds to me like you're actually a peace-loving, chicken-shit."

"I'm not a chicken-shit. But I'm just trying to figure why I'd want to take the risk. It wasn't my face that got punched."

"Okay."

"Besides, ruining a piece of heavy equipment wouldn't give you direct revenge on the guy that punched you."

"I know that, but even indirect revenge will make me feel better."

"I don't know, man . . ."

"Okay, see ya. Cluck. Cluck." I flapped my arms like chicken wings.

"Ah, what the hell. Let's book, I suppose what you have in mind is copasetic. And you did haul my ass into the hospital today."

Scallion Construction Company was building a huge new lawn, constructing a new flower garden, building a fountain, developing new contouring, and planting new trees and shrubs. It looked like it was going to be beautiful when they completed the job. And I supposed they were doing extensive work inside the temple as well.

Scallion had erected a fence around their equipment. They had stacks of building material inside the compound. They had machinery. They had a travel trailer used as a headquarters with the words Scallion Construction Company, Moab, Utah, stenciled along the side.

The fence was just for show. Scrotum and I just slipped under the bottom strand and there we were, standing in the middle of all sorts of expensive heavy equipment. It was slightly harder for Scrotum to get under the bottom rung because of his gimpy ankle and the crutches. He had finally decided it was best to use them.

They had one Pettibone, two tractors, three fork lifts, two generators, and one crane, but I selected a D8 Caterpillar Crawler to play a role in my play for revenge.

"Should we go buy some sugar?" Scrotum asked. "Just for grins we could dump it into the gas tank to see what happens."

"Negative. I have a better idea," I said.

"What?"

"I think I'll take this Cat for a little spin," I belched. "And when I get it crawling along on the outskirts of town I'll jump off and let it go." Hiccup.

"Righteous, dude, righteous," Scrotum said.

"You follow in the Ford and pick me up as soon as I get to the outskirts of St. George. I don't want to set it lose in the city and tear up innocent people's houses and shit."

"Are you serious about this?"

"As a case of the clap."

"What if you get caught? A Cat makes a hell of a racket."

"The people will just think there's a night crew out working construction. I'll just drive the Cat along like I'm on my way to an important job."

"What if you get caught?" Hiccup, burp.

"If I get caught, just take the Ford and go back to the dorm. Don't involve yourself, and never admit to a thing."

"You're psychotic, dude, psychotic."

"It's the wine."

"Bullshit, I've had more than you."

"Okay, have it your way. I'm crazy as a junk yard dog."

"You've got me trippin' just thinkin' about this, dude, trippin'" Scrotum said, laughing.

"Okay, let's get started." I climbed up on the Cat, started the engine and dropped it into gear. It crawled across the yard and walked through the fence like it was butter. Driving the beast was an adrenaline rush. But I managed to contain myself and throttle it back and let it crawl along at a reasonable pace. Its immense power thrummed through my body and thrilled me down to my toes.

I'd operated a smaller Cat, a Danata D4, the summer before, but I'd never taken the controls to a big Cat and felt such power. God, it was so cool. I'd spent last summer working with my neighbor, a lumberman, at a remote lumber camp in the Wasatch-Cache National Forest at a place named Smith and Morehouse. Brad Jensen, of Jensen Lumber Company, my neighbor, was a skilled Cat-skidder and he showed me how to skid timber using the little

Cat. We skidded tens of thousands of board feet of raw timber during the summer of 1961.

I crawled the big Cat out to 400 South and let it walk along the side of the road. I tried to avoid running it on the pavement to prevent damaging it which meant I had to walk the Cat over the mouth of several residential driveways and the corner of somebody's lawn; there just wasn't enough road edge left in those areas. I can't say why I chose to destroy private property rather than municipal property. Apparently the people who owned the driveways and the lawn were sound asleep or not at home, or I might have had somebody after me.

The going was slow, but I finally reached St. George's outskirts. I jumped off the Cat and let it go. Scrotum was there to pick me up. I let him drive The Drifter, but we decided that rather than speed off, that it would be cool to see what happens.

"If you get caught at this they'll be piping you sunshine for many a moon," he said.

"I know."

"I still don't see how this helps you get revenge against the guy that punched you in the face."

I shrugged. "I suppose it doesn't, but it'll hit his daddy in the pocketbook. It'll teach ol' man Scallion to spawn an imbecile for a son."

Scrotum looked at me and shook his head, and then he got into a laughing jag, hung his head out the window and barfed. "There, that helps with the nausea," he said, wiping at his mouth.

"That better not have splattered on the side of my Ford."

"Hey, dude, it might have splattered just a little."

"I wish I could barf myself. The world is spinning 'round and 'round. When I get in bed I'll probably have to put a foot on the floor to keep the room from spinning."

"Yeah, man, I know what you mean, I've done that."

"I shouldn't have drunk the wine. I've got my first classes tomorrow and I need to be sharp." My mind had come slightly out of the Mogen David induced fog and I began thinking a little more clearly.

Scrotum shook his head again. "Hey, man, let's not watch the Cat anymore and get the hell out of here. I need to go back to my room and throw out all the drunks and get some shuteye. I've got classes tomorrow, man."

"No. Let's watch what the Cat does before we call it a night."

"Don't you think it would be a good idea to get out of here?"

"Of course it would, but let's see what happens."

"It's your funeral. No, our funeral," he said, resigning himself to hanging around. He cut the lights on the Ford and we just sort of trailed along behind the Cat that was illuminated in the moonlight. It cut across an alfalfa field, walked through an irrigation canal, and then walked up a steep hillside and plowed through a farmer's barn. When it exited the far side of the barn it was pushing a tractor connected to a hay bailer before it. Finally the tractor and hay bailer got shoved broadside into a huge cottonwood tree and everything came to a momentary stop. The Cat's engine coughed and nearly stalled, but suddenly it caught and it walked up the side of the tractor and bailer to an almost vertical attitude, and then the nose came crashing down on the tree and broke it off about ten feet up. The tree toppled over onto the kitchen of a small, ranch-style home. It essentially cut the place in half. I assumed there was nobody in the kitchen; I hoped so, leastwise. But before long, lights winked on from two bedrooms at the far end of the house.

I was worried because I hadn't counted on there being homes after we left the outskirts of St. George. But there was a smattering of homes strung along the rural highway the Cat traversed.

The Cat just missed going in a front yard swimming pool, it caromed off a guardrail and walked right over somebody's new Ford Edsel. It smashed the Edsel into junk and continued down a farmer's lane. It tore its way through a small grain silo and continued on, piled high with wheat.

I'll never forget what happened next as it headed for the Virgin River. It was obvious the adventure was about to reach a conclusion, so Scrotum and I jumped out of the Ford and ran to the edge of the river. We wanted to be right up there to see it take the plunge. We did, and the moonlight lit it up nicely. The big Cat sailed off a fifty-foot embankment, and went nose down with wheat coming off it in streamers that looked sort of like the contrail coming off an airliner. It landed in the Virgin River, kersplash, and the water snuffed out the engine. When the dust, smoke, and water spray settled, all that was left was the back end of the D8 Cat poking up out of the water. It sort of looked as if it had gone bobbing for apples.

"Outta sight, man," Scrotum said.

I attended three classes the next day. But it hardly mattered because I flunked every class I took at Dixie Junior College during that first quarter.

That first day is etched in my mind because Audie Murphy was there to address the student body during an assembly. "Isn't that a funny thing about that D8 Cat being set loose last night?" he asked, giving us that wry little smile. "If one of you students is responsible for it, go to the authorities and confess. Don't worry; you can rise above the penalties you will pay for going crosswise to the law. You can still become a success in life's lottery—all is not lost. After all, this is America where anything is possible."

Shortly after, students leaped in to discuss the incident with the Cat, the destroyed house, the barn, the silo, the tractor and bailer, and the Edsel. It was on everyone's mind. Some dollar figures were mentioned that might possibly add up to the total in damages, but everybody came in low. The following day the paper said the damages came in at $150,000.

Then Murphy went on to talk about drama—Dixie had an excellent drama department. Then he told us about his role in World War II. He called a coed up on stage to use her for a prop and after a while when he asked her to return to her seat he leaned into her and gave her a kiss right on the lips. The rumor mill had it that she didn't wash her lips and walked around like a zombie for about a week until one of her friends told her to snap out of it.

I didn't have a clue about how to pass college-level courses. I started out by not bothering to read the lesson books, just somehow thinking the information would percolate into my mind through osmosis, or some other equally mysterious method.

But once I had that first quarter behind me, thank God, I learned how to study and truly learn.

I spent a little extra time retaking the classes I failed at Dixie Junior College and I went on to matriculate at the University of Utah. Eventually, I came away from the U. of U. with an MA in journalism. I decided to follow in my father's footsteps, even though he didn't love me.

But it didn't take long to realize that I wasn't going to get rich being a journalist, so I ended up in real estate. Now I own a small real estate firm in Kanab, Utah. Cummings' Realty has been a steady, if not sensational, earner for years. I have a lovely wife, Karen, and two children. We have pretty much lived the American Dream in what has to be the best state in the Union.

Forty years have passed since I loosed that Cat over in St. George. I have atoned for most all of my transgressions except for that one. So I sent Scallion Construction Company a check the other day, for $250,000. I adjusted the amount upward to cover interest and inflation. I also enclosed a letter confessing to the 1962 Caterpillar incident, but I didn't explain why I'd done it. There really wasn't a good reason to do that, and besides, the silly reason is embarrassing. The check was a money order and I put a fictitious name on it. Actually, I didn't want the kid, now an old guy like me, with the shredded physique finding me and punching me in the face again, because that had hurt like hell.

Scrotum killed himself in 1963. He overdosed on heroine and left a suicide note for his roommate. "Screw it," the note said. He was still attending DJC at the time. Dan Walton never finished college and he lives in Lehi, Utah. He's a long-haul trucker for Coors brewery. He hauls Coors from Golden Colorado into Salt Lake. He makes three trips a week. Surprisingly they drink a lot of beer in the Beehive State, right there in the shadow of the temple. I suspect that the gilded, twelve-foot bronze sculpture of the Angel Moroni, mounted atop the temple, is frowning, and it's not from a headache from blowing his horn vigorously. Dan and I stopped being friends after that first quarter at DJC. He said I was a lazy slob and a Siberian sack of sheep shit. I suppose he would've disliked me even more intensely if he'd known I was responsible for setting that Caterpillar loose.

In the end, I feel like Scallion Construction Company, kinda-sorta, received redress for my having wronged them forty years earlier. Now I am pretty much at peace with everything. So, hopefully, when I die I won't be sent to stoke furnaces and shit like that.

WINZE

It was January 21, 1961, and my friend, Joe Winterton, and I were listening to tunes on the car radio when they cut away and put on John F. Kennedy's inaugural speech. My name is Ken Applegate and I work for Covington Advertising in Salt Lake City, Utah. But I was born and raised in Park City, Utah, and that is were this story unfolds.

We were at the time of the Kennedy broadcast dragging Main Street in my '57 Chevrolet Bel Air. I'd left the little Chevy pretty much stock, because it was nice enough the way it came from the factory. All it had in the way of extras was baby moon hubcaps, a set of glass packs, oh, and a set of dump tubes that came out just behind the front wheels. But I hardly ever uncapped them because they were loud and obnoxious and they brought cops down on me like hordes of locust.

It was a bad-assed pussy wagon for its day.

Joe and I'd been friends going back to kindergarten. I loved the guy, I truly did. We bandied insults around like crazy and laughed about it, but woe unto anyone else who dared to insult one of us, the other would be to his defense in an instant. We were listening to Wolfman Jack on KOMA, broadcast out of Oklahoma City with 50,000 watts of energy. It was jokingly said that KOMA had enough power to reach Mars. I don't know about that, but I do know it had easily enough power to reach us out in Park City, Utah.

Back in those days I was a hard-rock miner, yet, even then, I was a hopeless political junky. I got caught up in Kennedy's speech. Kennedy had won a close race against Richard Nixon. Earlier that day Kennedy had attended the Holy Trinity Catholic Church in Georgetown. Then later he had ridden along accompanied by Ike Eisenhower to the east front of the capitol building for the inaugural ceremony. It was a nasty, blustery day, but Kennedy insisted they proceed with the outdoor ceremony, weather be damned. Eventually he took the oath of office from Chief Justice Warren and then he launched into his stem-winder speech that was to become a national icon. It made me proud to be an American. "And so my fellow Americans—ask not what the country can do for you—ask what you can do for your country." I admired Kennedy, even if he was a Democrat.

"Kennedy is a goddamn faggot," Joe said, pissed because they'd preempted his precious Wolfman Jack. "We'd be better off if Richard Nixon would've won."

"Bullshit, Tricky Dick should never be voted into any office, ever, even if he is a Republican. The man's not fit to be a dogcatcher, let alone the leader of the free world."

"Bullshit."

"Bullshit? Okay, scrote, tell me why Tricky Dick should get the top job in the free world?"

"I don't have a reason. I just feel it in my bones."

"Spoken like a true liberal who approaches political matters by feeling, rather than by intellect. Geez. Drink your beer will ya, and stay away from politics because you don't know your ass from a hole in the ground."

"Flake off, man. I suppose you think you know all about politics?"

"More than you, needledick."

"Ha, you'll think needledick. I have to push this thing around in a wheel barrow to get 'er up off the ground."

I laughed. "You're delusional."

Wolfman Jack's gravelly voice suddenly crackled to life through the radio speakers.

"Good, Wolfman's back," Joe said. "You're right, screw politics. Let's listen to Jack. Incidentally, Sue Ellen sent word to thank you for the mining job you set up for me. She's been really worried about money, what with a new baby coming and all."

I worked underground over in Keetley, Utah. I was a hard rock miner like my daddy. Daddy was the day shift foremen at the United Park City Mines Company, headquartered in Keetley. Daddy had agreed to hire Joe. The U.P.C.M.C. had mines scattered all over Keetley and Park City, and I think up in Kellogg, Idaho; it was a fairly large mining company. In later years they diversified and began developing the skiing industry there in Park City which led to the whole Park City ski resort thing. Much later, I was promoted to a job above-ground, clearing ski trails and surveying the path for a ski gondola that traveled to the top of the Wasatch Range.

Dad got me a job in the mine two years earlier, shortly after I'd graduated from Park City High School. Many of my friends had gone off to Brigham Young University, the University of Utah, Utah State, and other colleges in Utah.

But not me, because I'd decided to try mining for a while and see if somewhere down the line I might develop a yen for higher learning. I realized I didn't have to be a miner forever.

"Hey spaz, how dangerous is this mining racket?"

"As dangerous as all hell, but you learn to just not think about it. But, quite frankly, there are a whole lot of ways to get dead or badly injured in a mine."

"Crikey."

"Will you stop saying 'crikey'?"

"It's just a slang version of Christ. I say it because it's not really cussin'" he said, tongue in cheek.

"Ha, like that would matter to you. So, are you scared of working in the mine?"

"Yeah, I am."

"Well, get over it, candyass. You've got to take care of that new bride and baby."

Joe looked a little pale as he took a slurp of his Coors. "Are you jerkin' me off?"

I laughed. "No, it really is dangerous. Accordin' to the Bureau of Labor Statistics, mining is number one on the top ten list of the most dangerous jobs in America. It's even more dangerous than highway construction and commercial fishin'."

"How do you know?"

"I read the newspaper. Don't you?"

"No."

"That's sad."

"I don't know about this mining shit. Maybe I don't want to work underground. I could get a job at a dairy farm over in Heber."

"Ah, come on, what a candyass. The mine pays good money and the hours are good."

We had been going up and down Main Street for nearly an hour and there wasn't much going on. Specifically, we were out cruising for women and there weren't any out. Joe had proclaimed that he was true to his relatively new spouse. He had only been married three months. But if opportunity knocked I knew ol' Joe would happily succumb to his baser instincts. Joe had a sex drive that was truly one of the great wonders of the world.

"Maybe we should cruise over to Heber and see what's goin' on. I could sure use a little poontang, couldn't you?"

"Knock it off, will ya? I'm a married man."

"You mean to say you'd let a little thing like a marriage certificate get in the way of a good time? Even if some gal just threw it up in your face?"

"Crikey. Little Sue Ellen would kill me."

"Ah, Joe, it's not nice to horseshit your old granddad."

We were just making our turn-around at the top of Main Street, a steep incline that cuts a track through Park City's business district: small grocery stores, hardware stores, clothing outlets, a movie theater, restaurants, and a disproportionate number of bars. Jenny Anderson, the town punchboard, was on her porch with another punchboard named Brenda Barns. They had a little radio out there blaring Elvis Presley singing "Stranger in Paradise." They were working some hula hoops and their hips were rocking back and forth provocatively.

The girls were in jeans and bulky sweaters because it was a little nippy out that night. When Jenny saw me she stopped her hula hoop and stuck out a leg, meant to entice me to stop and pick them up.

But I ignored her—my sights were set higher that night. Besides, I'd had Jenny's drawers down around her ankles just the night before and it hadn't been pleasant. She should consider springing for an aerosol container of feminine hygiene spray. Anyway, there wasn't much of a challenge there. All a man need do is stick a tongue in her ear and she'd roll over backward on those round heels and offer up the Promised Land. Now what kind of satisfaction is there to be gotten there? I like working for it a little. I gave Jenny the finger, "Climb it, Tarzan," I said, but she really didn't hear it. Then I made the U-turn and headed back down Main. I goosed the old Chevy, dropped her into low gear and let her back rap. Those glass packs cackled pretty as you please and life seemed good.

"Thanks for not stoppin'," Joe said. "This is a small town and I know that word would get back to little Sue Ellen. Not to mention I'd've probably ended up with a case of the clap."

"I hope to find some better stuff for us," I said.

"No, just tell me more about the mine. Let's just cruise and slam a few more Coors and talk mining."

"Okay, story time. Dad said that in the olden days they used draft horses to pull the ore cars along the tracks down in the mines. The Park City mining district is honeycombed with mines, some originating back to the eighteen-hundreds, hollowed out slick by horsepower."

"No shit?"

"No shit, needledick. Once a horse was lowered underground they never brought it back up to daylight. It stayed down there until it died of overwork."

Johnny Mathis came over the speakers with, "What Will My Mary Say?"

"Crikey," Joe said, after listening to Johnny for a few moments.

"Really. To this day, chunks of horse hair are wedged in the cracks along the tunnel walls."

"That bites."

"Doesn't it? Nowadays we tug the ore cars around with electric motors powered by overhead copper cables, kind of like the trolley cars in San Francisco."

"Is it possible to get electrocuted down there?"

I laughed. "Yeah, it could happen."

"That doesn't sound too cool. How'd they get the horses down the shafts? Horses are too long. Aren't those shafts just five by five feet square?"

"They'd lower the horses slung underneath the cages. They'd put slings beneath the horse's bellies. The horse would fold up and go right down the shaft pretty as you please. Except for those times when the sling wasn't set right. Then they'd plunge two thousand feet or so to their deaths."

"Bummer."

"Yeah, it was a bummer. The poor horses wouldn't drop straight down, you know, and go Ker plunk on the bottom. They'd hit timbers and bounce into the various levels on the way down, loosing body parts as they went. I guess their parts were found here and there for thousands of feet along the downward path."

"Crikey."

"Tell me about it. And get this, during the Great Depression a man jumped down the shaft up at the Judge—he'd been lookin' for work for months and he'd just been turned back yet again there at the Judge. I guess they found parts of him scattered all the way down. How'd you have liked to have been on that clean-up detail?"

"That would've sucked, too, but it would've sucked even worse being the poor bastard that made the leap."

"Yeah. Now, about timber gases—they're something else you need to know about."

"Timber gases?"

"Yeah, the old timbers, after decades of being damp, begin to decay, lettin' out carbon dioxide, which is a deadly gas."

"Can you smell the stuff?"

"No, it just creeps up on you and kills you deader'n a door nail. Dad climbed up on a muck pile one time and stuck his head through a little opening to shine his light down the tunnel on the other side, just to see what was there. Timber gas hit him. It'd been trapped on the other side where there hadn't been any ventilation. He conked out and slid back down the muck pile on his back. It was quite a spell before he came to."

Wolfman Jack came on and announced Booker T and the MGs singing "Twist and Shout." Joe wanted to get out of the car and practice the twist.

I wouldn't stop to let him. I thought the twist was a silly-looking dance practiced by candyasses. "Only candyasses do the twist," I said.

I reached over and turned the station and plunked us right into the middle of Frankie Avalon singing "Venus."

"You like Frankie Avalon?" Joe asked.

"He's all right."

"What else have you got to tell about the mining racket?"

"When I first began working in the mine last year I worked with my ol' man. He hadn't been made foreman yet."

"And?"

"I was down on the twelve-hundred-foot level up in the Sperry Tunnel. I was running a motor that day and I had the motor sitting right in front of the shaft and I was standing alongside it. Dad was running another motor and he was up around a bend in the tunnel."

"Outta sight, man. This tale has me right on the edge of my seat."

"Okay, wiseass, I'm not finished yet, and you know that I'm not." I took a deep breath to get control so that I could resist slapping my old pal up alongside the head.

"And so?" Joe asked. "Then what happened?" Joe said, letting his tongue loll out and panting like a dog. I loved Joe, but he could be a wiseass from time to time.

"Dad came flyin' around the bend, his motor speeding along flat out. The power arm had jumped off the copper power line and he was out of control without brakes or power, and he couldn't jump off the motor because the tunnel walls had him hemmed in."

"Outta sight, man, then what went down?"

"So, he was without question going to crash into my motor, knock it down the shaft and follow behind it. Remember what I told you about those horses and that Depression era suicide victim?"

"What happened?"

"I threw my motor into reverse and sent it up the tunnel on a collision course, and, yeah, by God, there was a helluva collision. It really shook the old man up, but it saved his bacon."

"I bet he was pissed, if I know your ol' man . . . even if you did save his bacon."

"Hell, yeah, he was pissed, super pissed. He asked me why I didn't come up with a better plan. But after he thought about it he realized there wasn't a better plan, and that he owed me his life. But he could never bring himself to thank me; all he did was piss and moan about his bruises."

Mary Sue Sunbloom, a mousy little sophomore attending Park City High, was strolling along in front of the old municipal library. She was holding a miniature radio up to her ear and rocking out to music. I edged the Chevy up next to her and Joe reached out and goosed her right in the behind. It looked to me like her jump was near to being a world's record. We edged on down the road, laughing. I looked in the rearview mirror and her lips were flapping to beat the band.

Joe took a huge swig of Coors and we cruised on. We had demolished the better part of a case and we weren't feeling much pain. Joe had been married going on three months and it was the first time little Sue Ellen had let him out of her sight.

"So, I suppose you have a few more mining tales?"

"Yeah, I do," I said. "A couple weeks ago I was working the Grizzly up in the Judge. It was my job to hook a motor to a string of loaded mining cars and pull them up alongside the Grizzly, which is a row of steel slats set into the ground and spaced four inches apart. I had to dump the ore out of each car onto the Grizzly and bust the boulders up with a sledgehammer so that every piece would slip down between the slats. It made the ore easier to transport."

"How'd you dump the cars? Weren't they heavy?"

"Ungodly heavy. The cars are side-dumps and the dumping is done with a lever. But the cars also have a chain and hook attachment used to keep the entire car from falling down onto the grizzly. If you work the grizzly, make sure you seat the hook at the end of the chain firmly into the bolt that is fastened to the tunnel wall."

"Or the car will tumble down onto the grizzly?"

"Yeah, that and the fact the chain will wrap around your head and the hook will smack you in the chops. The hook will knock out a shitload of your teeth."

"You're hammered, you've drank too much—my *teeth*?"

"Yeah, and here is why I know it will happen. I showed up at the Grizzly one morning and there was blood and teeth scattered all over the place. Sapo Tomlinson, who was on the graveyard shift the night before, failed to fasten the hook into the ring bolt properly and when he side-dumped the car the chain came flying at him like a bullet and smacked him right in the face. It knocked out most of his front teeth and fractured his jaw. He's not exactly handsome anymore."

"Crikey. I don't know about this mining business."

"You're such a candyass."

About that time Jimmy Barnes putt-putted by us on his motor scooter. There was no snow that winter and Jimmy liked riding his scooter; the guy was a total loser.

"Run that sumbitch over," Joe said. "I've hated him ever since grade school. He's such a pussy and he thinks he's better than everybody else. You know he's a doctor's son from a rich family and probably a faggot?"

I put the hammer down on the Ford and those glass packs were bellowing to beat the band. I come flying up on Jimmy Barnes riding his scooter and I dropped the Ford down into low gear and let 'er back-rap. It scared Jimmy really bad because he opened up the throttle on his Moped, I think it was a Moped, or some other dorky little scooter, and he got serious about getting to his garage before I ran him down. I stayed right on his tail until he got to his driveway and then I backed off a little to let the scared little twit make the turn into his driveway. But he tried to take the turn too fast and lay the scooter down. It skidded along on its side and Jimmy was on his behind skidding right along behind it until he ran astraddle a mailbox post and crushed the family jewels.

"Crikey!" Joe said, which started us roaring with laughter.

"Will you stop saying that crikey shit," I said, laughing and snorting. Well, here's the thing, at that point we both laughed until Joe's stomach got to acting up and his gag reflex kicked in. When I let him out to ralph, I kept up the laughing and came close to ralphing myself, all over my steering wheel and suicide knob with naked ladies in provocative poses.

Joe climbed back in and wiped his mouth.

"Joe, let's call it a night," I said. I'd given up on chasing any women down, and tomorrow was another day.

"I thought you had more mining stories. Hey, man, no foolin', this mining really scares me. I'm too young to die."

"I know, Joe, but you're not going to die. Everything will be fine."

"See ya tomorrow, scrote," Joe said, climbing out of the Ford.

"You're the only scrote I know. *Mañana.* I'll pick you up at five in the morning."

"God, that's only three hours from now."

Three hours later I drove into Joe's driveway and Sue Ellen stepped out on the porch and told me that Joe had gotten up early and headed for Heber. "He said that mining is too dangerous, that he's going to get a job milking cows for one of the dairy farmers over in Heber Valley."

"You married a candyass, Sue Ellen."

"Hey, watch it," Sue Ellen said as I roared off. "He's not a candyass."

That night Joe called and said he couldn't get work with a dairy farmer over in Heber, and that he was ready to give mining a try after all.

"The old man's pissed, but I suppose if you show up tomorrow he'll still let you hire on."

The next morning I picked up Joe and drove him up to the Sperry tunnel. I marched him into the superintendent's office and helped get him signed on.

Then I shepherded him to the dressing room and showed him how to don the diggers for hard-rock mining. All of the mining employee's diggers were on hooks and spooled up to the ceiling on chains. Mines are wet places and the diggers are always wet and everything seems to dry better hoisted up to the ceiling.

Joe took down a set of diggers that'd belonged to a guy who'd quit a few days earlier. The former employee had had a close call. Apparently a set of timbers had let loose and he'd been grazed by a boulder as big as a Volkswagen. He'd been pulling the chute down on the 800 foot level when the roof let loose above him. After that close-call he'd been hauled into the hospital over in Heber with extensive bruising, and luckily that's all. Regardless, he'd decided to pack it in.

After we got dressed I took him to the battery room for his headlamp and battery pack, I showed him how to strap the battery pack to his belt and the light to his hard-hat. So there Joe stood in his diggers, with nothing on underneath but his underwear . . . that's the way it's done. It gets damn hot down there. If the miners wore clothes they'd die of the heat. He didn't like the idea of going into the mine in nothing but his skivvies and rubber outerwear.

"I feel like I'm naked," Joe said.

"You are, for all practical purposes," I said.

"Are there any queers working in this mine?"

"No, but some of them seem like they are."

"What?"

"You'll see."

We climbed into a man-train packed with miners that started squirting each other with rubber squeeze bottles, cracking each other's knuckles, and goosing one another. Joe got squirted right square in the face with a stream of water from one of the squirt bottles, then he had his fingers squeezed and mashed to see if they would pop, and then he got goosed dead center in the testicles—expertly done by a gnarled old miner with grime in his pores from decades of mining and too few baths.

"Welcome to our world, son, welcome," the old fellow said.

113

"What'n the hell is wrong with you, you old fool? I'm going to kick your faggot ass," Joe said, balling up his fists.

I had to stop Joe from taking a poke at the old guy. If he had done that he'd've gone on everybody's shit list and ruined his job. It was just better to go along with the testicle-crushing and hope for the best. The goosing thing was an everyday occurrence around the Park City mining district. The miners weren't gay, they had wives and girlfriends. They just got their jollies crushing one another's testicles. It was accepted practice in their subterranean world. Most were probably afflicted with just a touch of sadism. If a miner got a good purchase on another miner's family jewels and got the victim begging, everybody had a huge laugh.

Once we rode back in the mountain a ways the motorman reached up and pulled a cord hanging from the ceiling and pneumatic batwing doors up ahead swung open, allowing us passage. On the other side the motorman pulled another cord and the doors swung shut, holding all of the fresh air inside the mine.

Fresh air was necessary to sustain life in those underground passages. The air was blown down a shaft sunk from the top of the mountain. A huge fan was perched up there on top of the mountain and blew downward into the maze of tunnels, winzes, slopes, and shafts.

After a short time we arrived at the staging station and stood in groups to be lowered down in the elevator to the various work levels. Joe was assigned to my work team and we were working a winze on the 1,300-foot level. Joe got goosed a few more times standing there on the platform waiting for the elevator.

"Joe, how's that young poontang you married, nice and tight, is it?" the gnarly old miner who'd assaulted him earlier asked.

Joe balled up his fist and was fixing to take a poke at the guy once again until I calmed him down. "Something else you'll have to get used to." I whispered in Joe's ear. "No subject is off-limits to these guys."

"That's none of your goddamn business," Joe did manage to say to the old miner, causing half a dozen miners to snort and laugh. They were enjoying themselves immensely, tormenting the new guy.

I tried to explain to Joe what a winze was and what our jobs would be when we arrived at the mouth of the beast. "A winze is driven down at a forty-five degree angle. It's like a shaft that has tipped over on an angle."

"What do we do?"

"We ride the skid bucket to the very bottom of it and clean up the muck created down there by the round of dynamite set there by the shift before us."

"Why?"

"To fill the skid bucket full of very valuable minerals, and to extend the depth of the winze to keep dropping lower to recover even more minerals."

"I'm not gettin' in that damned skid bucket." He shined his light down the winze. "I can't even see the bottom of this thing. What if that skinny-assed cable breaks?"

The air smelled dank and sort of earthy as it wafted up out of the winze.

"It won't. It lifts tons and tons of ore and waste up from the very bottom, which is, incidentally, seven hundred feet below. With just you and me in the skid bucket, the cable will hardly know we're there."

"What if the last few giant loads of ore strained the thing and it is just holding by a couple strands?"

"It hasn't been strained. The cable is fine. They inspect the thing every week. Very few miners have taken a ride to hell down one of these winzes. See how the skid bucket has wheels and rides on those rails mounted to timbers? Hey, it's safe, it's on wheels that are riding on smooth rails. It isn't dragging along in cracks and crevises."

"Yeah."

"Well, if the cable breaks there're spring-loaded dogs that open up and dig into those timbers the rails are mounted to."

"Do the dogs really bite in, and work?"

"No, they just slide along on the wet, slimy timbers."

"Crikey. There you go. I'm not getting in the sumbitch. That's not a very big cable, now, is it?"

"Get in, you candyass, we've got work to do. We gotta clean up the muck from the last shift, drill, set a round, and blow it so the shift after us can do their jobs."

Joe finally got in the skid bucket and we went down and did our job. Joe was a quick learner and he did a good job for being green.

Two days later when Joe was working at the bottom of the winze with Carl Widdison, I was up on the 300-foot level runnin' a muckin' machine at the time, he called the skid bucket down and got to daydreaming and forgot to signal the hoist man when to stop. It came down and crushed both Joe and Carl Widdison against the bottom of the winze. It was heavily loaded with new timbers. They were both killed instantly.

Losing Joe changed my life. I miss him to this day. I'd been a wild fool up until Joe's death. I was foul-mouthed, and disrespectful and disdainful of everyone and everything. But now I am different. I don't have problems looking at my mug in the mirror when I shave. Losing a close friend like that can have a sobering effect. I gave up mining and I work for Covington Advertising in Salt Lake. I just got involved in what we call a saturation advertising campaign to promote the 2002 Winter Olympics held in Salt Lake, with venues in nearby Park City and Heber. I made some serious coin working on that particular campaign. Advertising has been good to me. I've never married. I guess it just isn't for me.

Little Sue Ellen remarried and seems to be quite happy these days. I think she has seven children now, it's a Mormon thing. I see her in the grocery store occasionally and I marvel at the amount of groceries it takes to feed all those mouths. We talk about Joe and cry a little. She has forgiven me for the part I played in Joe's death, but I have never really forgiven myself.

SASQUINA

Sasquina Accawinna sat on a stool in a meadow with an artist's easel placed firmly before her. A Monarch butterfly flitted about at her feet and she could smell sagebrush and the pleasant aroma of meadow clover.

Her father, whom she always called *apé*—pronounced "top" in the Shoshone language—was in a nearby hayfield working a plot of land deeded to him and the Shoshone clan out of guilt by the white man, operating a clunky hay-mowing machine pulled behind two Percheron draft horses.

Paco Accawinna was a full-blooded Goshute Indian. The Goshutes, once the people of the great Shoshone Nation, inhabited a narrow strip of land in Western Utah that bordered the eastern Nevada state line, and had once been part of the ancient Shoshone hunting grounds. The tribe had been deeded 34,650 acres in 1911 and would get a great many more in 1914, which eventually rounded out to 111,000 acres. All of the land was to become known as the Goshute Indian Reservation.

Paco Accawinna had been taught ranching by the Mormon people. He was happy they had done so, so he had a trade that provided for the Accawinnas now that the ability to hunt and gather had been taken from the Shoshone people.

A slight breeze riffled the meadow grass around Sasquina's feet as she painted, and rustled the leaves on a nearby cottonwood tree. It was hot. Sasquina glanced at the desert that stretched before her and the heat waves that squiggled on the horizon. It was a splendid day. The air was clean and pure, and it had that familiar scent of desert aridity.

It smelled like home to Sasquina.

The Indian child was a tiny creature with coal black hair and the swarthy complexion of the full-blooded Shoshone. She had bright little eyes, dark as India ebony that twinkled with a lively intelligence — at the age of eight, she was already confident that someday her landscape portraits would hang in places like the Washington National Museum, the British Museum, and the Louvre. She knew she could make it happen.

Five years earlier, Sasquina had picked up a paint brush and started dabbing it on a canvas. She had watched her mother, who dabbled with paints from time to time, and she'd decided to give it a try. Before long she'd started drawing the flora and fauna she saw around her. Her parents had recognized her talent early on. They'd taken the long trip by horse and carriage on the Lincoln Highway Association into Salt Lake to buy their precocious child proper painting supplies.

Ibapah was the nearest community to their Deep Creek ranch. It was a loose collection of homes and shops, tucked up against the Oquirrh Mountains—a Goshute Indian word pronounced as "ochre" and meaning "wooded mountain"—but the Accawinnas were happy it existed, small or not. It saved them from driving the horse and carriage all the way to Wendover or Salt Lake City for household supplies.

The tiny community was located a hundred and twenty road-miles west of Salt Lake City. To get to Ibapah, people still used horse-drawn carriages, or drove one of those new-fangled automobiles west on the newly built Lincoln Highway, simply a dirt tract, but part of a road system that went from coast to coast.

Motorists carried several spare tires and parts in their cars in those days; a pothole could wreck the family Flivver. The traveler would leave the Lincoln Highway Association in Wendover, and double-back on another dirt tract for another twenty miles, easterly, to Ibapah, the closest settlement to the Accawinna's ranch.

As Sasquina sat there amid the clover, buttercups, and peppermint plants along a nearby ditch bank, she painted Ibapah Peak, looming majestically before her. The mountain jutted 12,087 feet into rarefied air and stood slightly taller than Mt. Nebo in Juab County, slightly shorter than Kings

Peak, and Kings Peak South, in Summit County up in the Uintahs, the four tallest peaks in Utah. The piece of artwork was nearly complete and Sasquina with seeming ease had captured Ibapah Peak's splendid dignity.

Right at noon, Paco drove up to Sasquina on the horse-drawn hay mower and stepped down. "I have brought us *guchumunduku* for lunch," Paco said, laughing.

"Apé, you're silly. What's that?"

"That's Shoshone for beef."

"It seems easier just to call it beef. Is it really lunch time and do you really have beef?"

"Take the *bungus* to *baá*, would you, Sasquina?"

"You mean take the horses to water?"

"Yeah. Got to keep you fluent in Shoshone words."

Sasquina took the team to the creek for water. She marveled at their size and beauty. "Is it lunch time?" she asked when she returned.

"Yeah, it's lunch time, Sasquina," he said, "and yeah, I have beef sandwiches, salted crackers, and water, and a slice of cherry pie your *biá* baked."

"That sounds good, Apé. Thank you for bringing me with you."

"You're welcome. You know I always enjoy having my little Sasquina by my side."

"Come and look at what I've done on my painting. How does it look?"

Paco stepped over and behind her to look over her shoulder. He was stunned by what he saw. He was so proud he nearly burst the buttons on his denim work shirt. "Sasquina, you've done a wonderful job on this one. It looks just like the mountain."

"Thank you, *Apé*. I love you, *Apé*."

"I love you, too, Sasquina," Paco said, giving her a kiss on the cheek. "The painting is good, but you've left out a few items, like those huge boulders, the brush, and the dead falls."

"That's one of the rules of painting landscapes: You should only put in those items that make the picture better."

Paco continued studying the picture. "And what about these items you painted in that aren't really there?"

"Daddy, unless it's a scene everybody knows, as the landscape artist I can paint in whatever I want if it makes the portrait better."

Paco walked over to the hay mower and pulled a rucksack loose from behind the seat. It held their lunch. When he returned he had another question. "Why is it that you've painted the items that are closer more in detail?"

"That's what I have learned reading the book you and Biá bought me," Sasquina said, giggling. "The viewer's eye just naturally goes to the front of a picture."

"You're a smart little girl, aren't you? Sasquina, I'm so proud of you. Imagine a full-blooded Shoshone Indian maiden painting such nice pictures."

"Remember, I'm a Goshute Indian now, not Shoshone. And remember, I still have more to learn about painting, but I am close to reaching my potential."

"Perhaps you do, Sasquina, but the pictures you paint look fine to me."

"Thank you, *Apé*"

Paco pointed to some green sagebrush she'd painted in, stretching along the foothills of Ibapah Peak. It was darker and more muted than the other greens. "How did you get that color?"

"I just mixed in a little black with a shade of green from a tube."

"Yeah, I understand. You mixed *duhubite* with *buhubite,* as the Shoshone would say."

"It is easier saying black and green in English; they are shorter words."

"Maybe. But we shouldn't forget our Shoshone ways."

"I'm hungry, *Apé*. Can we eat now?"

They ate and soaked up the early afternoon sunshine and surveyed their domain. If the white men had taken the time to look at the acreage they'd deeded over to the Goshute people, at how beautiful it was, they might have had a change of heart.

Sasquina had been born in 1904, right there in Deep Creek, at a spot later named Ibapah. She was proud of her lineage, and much like the rest of the Goshute people, she was angry and distrustful of the white man, but one would never know it judging by her demeanor. She always wore a huge smile.

Sasquina's *biá* and *apé*, Kimama—butterfly—and Paco had gotten married in 1901 and they'd moved into the ranch house that was nestled right up against the Oquirrh Mountains, separating them from the Great Salt Lake Valley. Paco had already taken possession of the small ranch, which was why he'd permitted himself to take a bride.

After the marriage, Paco Accawinna struggled with the cattle operation for two years before he learned how to make it pay. After that he'd eked out a meager living, breeding cattle. A lot of his beef was sold to the army base at Fort Douglas, located on the eastern foothills of Salt Lake City. Kimama kept urging him to give up the ranch and move five miles deeper into the Goshute Indian Reservation. She wanted to be closer to her parents, the Tendoys, who were direct descendents of Chief Tendoy of the Lemhi Mountain Shoshones in Idaho. "We could move into a cabin my *apé* owns, live for free, and run sheep," Kimama said.

But Paco didn't want to run sheep. "My people have always run sheep, going back to when the buffalo disappeared. I want to run cattle."

In the end, Paco won the debate and ran his cattle business successfully until 1914. Sasquina loved living on the ranch. There was so much to see and so much to do, so many things to paint, like Muley deer and bobcats that came down from the mountains to drink in the ranch's pond.

During those cattle-ranch days the Accawinnas didn't get rich, but they held it together. They occasionally had venison and beef for their dinner table, and fresh vegetables from a small garden adjacent to the ranch house.

Ranch life was thrilling to Sasquina. Coyotes howled in the evenings and it never failed to stir her in a primal way, and give her chill bumps. Thus went her life, a daily communion with the natural world there at Deep Creek and her never-ending and exciting quest to become a very capable landscape artist. Her parents just let her roam about and paint, as long as she handled her ranch chores first.

In 1914 World War I broke out in Europe and Uncle Sam decided the Goshutes qualified for the draft. There were one hundred able-bodied

Goshute braves, but they were advised by tribal council not to register, that they weren't constrained by law to do so.

Not knowing this was the reaction, the army dispatched a young Salt Lake physician from Fort Douglas to Ibapah to give the Goshutes their physicals. His name was Larry Jensen and he wasn't a bad sort, he was just carrying out a job for a fee.

Not one of the one hundred braves, including Paco, showed up for their physicals; Chief Joe showed up as their proxy.

"Why do ya wanna kill Germans?" Chief Joe asked.

"Because they sank one of America's ships, the *Lusitania*, and Germany is trying to take over all its neighbors." Jensen replied.

"If Americans would stay home they wouldn't get sunk."

"Are you going to call in the hundred braves or not? America needs them."

"Nope! A war in Europe ain't our problem."

"Why not?"

"Goshutes aren't American citizens. We have our own separate nation here. You're draft is evil."

"Maybe so, but those braves still have to register."

"No," Chief Joe repeated.

"What about pride in your nation?"

"Ha! Pride? In the nation run by pale faces that destroyed our lives, took our land? Pride? White eyes, you're on loco weed. 'Sides, we've got no quarrel with the Germans."

"It's your patriotic duty to help America fight," Jensen insisted.

"We won't fight. If the Germans had come in here'n sank one of our canoes we would fight. But they didn't."

"But the Germans sank the *Lusitania* and American men and women were killed," Jensen said.

"Good. Serves them right."

Jensen went back to Salt Lake having failed to give the Goshutes medical examinations for the draft. It was particularly galling because he didn't receive the fifty dollar fee he'd stood to earn.

Shortly after that, two hundred soldiers were sent out by the 20ᵗʰ Infantry at Fort Douglas with orders to arrest the five members of the Goshute Tribal Council for refusing to allow the Goshute tribal members to register for the draft. When they arrived in Ibapah, they discovered all one hundred braves had fled after cleaning out the general store of all ammunition. It was rumored that they'd headed to the Oquirrhs to take a stand.

The troops headed for the mountain without delay. They drove their trucks to within a few miles and hiked the rest of the way to the base of the Oquirrhs. There was only one Goshute at that spot: Paco Accawinna. He'd been left behind to communicate with the troops because he spoke the best English. He'd been left behind to try to turn the U.S. troops back.

"The Goshute tribal councilmen couldn't find a suitable spot near the Oquirrhs to take a stand, so they moved on to Skull Valley," Paco told the troops.

"Why did you stay behind?" a young lieutenant named Jerry Barns asked.

"To talk to you."

"Reason with us?" Barns asked.

"Yeah. Won't you please turn around and go back to Salt Lake and leave the Goshute people alone?"

"The Goshutes have to register for the draft; that's United State's law," Barns stated.

"Let me show you something that proves we don't have to register for the draft."

When he reached into his pocket, a PFC named Dial Kemmer shot Paco through the torso with a Model 17 Enfield. Paco was dead before he hit the ground.

Lieutenant Barns rushed over and yanked the Enfield out of the young soldier's hands and gave him a resounding slap across the face. "You fool, why did you shoot him?"

"Sir, I thought he was reaching for a weapon."

"A weapon? You damn fool. Couldn't you see he was a peaceful Indian?"

"Sorry."

"Sorry don't cut it." Barns looked at several nearby troops. "Place PFC Kemmer under arrest. Put a set of manacles on him and we'll transport him back to Fort Douglas to face a General Courts Martial." He looked at Kemmer with contempt. "I hope you get the firing squad."

"A General Courts Martial, sir? A firing squad?" Big tears welled up in Kemmer's eyes.

"Yeah. That Indian was merely reaching for a document to prove his case. The document wasn't there, but that's what he was about."

"I'm sorry."

"Sorry's not good enough. You've murdered this Indian, *murdered* him. Let's go home, men, and leave these Goshute's alone. World War One really isn't their problem."

The proof that Paco claimed to have proving that Goshutes weren't eligible for the draft was never found. There were rumors that one of the soldiers, hoping to protect his pal Kemmer, secretly lifted it from Paco's pocket and destroyed the damning document. But this remains to be merely supposition.

Lieutenant Barns faced a General Courts Martial for disobeying an order, by refusing to round up the Goshutes for conscription into Uncle Sam's army. He told the panel at the courts martial that his "conscience got in the way of duty." He was fined heavily and dismissed from the service with a dishonorable discharge. Six months later he died of a lung disease. But he had saved the Goshutes; because the army let the issue die.

PFC Dial Kemmer was found guilty of murder and his sentence carried out by a firing squad.

The following day, Chief Joe rode up to the Accawinnas ranch house and tied his bay mare to a piñon tree. Kimama Accawinna stepped out on the porch to see what he wanted. "Did the soldiers from Fort Douglas catch up with our braves?" she asked.

"No."

"Good. Did Paco do a good job finding a hidey-hole for the group? He knows the Oquirrhs like the back of his hand."

"No problem there."

She grew impatient. "Well, Chief Joe, why are you here?"

"Paco was kilt, Kimama. He was shot through the heart by one of those white devils."

Kimama lunged at him and tried to slap his face, but he caught her arm and held on to it until she stopped struggling. Then she commenced wailing like a wounded animal. The wailing touched Chief Joe's heart and the racket brought Sasquina out to the porch.

Then Kimama left off with the wailing and went to crying. Between sobs she managed to say, "You bastard, Joe, if you hadn't asked Paco to find all those cowards a hidey-hole, he'd still be alive."

"Kimama—"

"Shut up! Why didn't you just order all those braves to register for the draft, just order them . . .?"

"'Cause we're not U.S. citizens. The Goshute Indian reservation is sort of a separate nation, that's why."

When Sasquina realized her *apé* was dead, she started in with some crying of her own. "*Apé* is dead? No . . . no. Now who will love me? Take care of me? Go on horse rides with me? Make me sandwiches? Look at my portraits? Who?"

She broke out into tears, and this, too, broke Chief Joe's heart. He was nearly crying himself and he was supposed to be a big strong Indian Chief. Both were making such a racket that Chief Joe could hardly think. "Uh . . . uh . . . listen, just ride into Ibapah. His body is at the old Pony Express station. Uh . . . you need to come in to take care of his remains. I'm sorry . . . I'm sorry!" He backed off their porch and made his escape. He could hear their wailing above the clip-clop-clip of the bay's hoofs, until he dropped over a hogback into a saddle filled with Utah juniper and sagebrush. He reached up and wiped a couple tears that had leaked out of the corner of his eyes. He convinced himself that he really wasn't crying; that his eyes were just leaking a little . . . It was the damned wind.

The following morning, Kimama loaded Sasquina into their wagon and they headed into the trading post to take possession of Paco's body.

Chief Joe was there at the trading post. "Sign this death document and you can take Paco along with you." He stood considering something for a short period of time. "Uh, Kimama, this is against the white man's law, taking Paco away like this. He should be handled by a funeral home and buried the white man's way. But since we're out here in the desert, just take him and bury him in the tradition of the *newe* . . . The Shoshone way. The whites murdered him, so you can bury him anyway you see fit. That's the way I see it."

Kimama signed the document and Chief Joe and a simple-minded Goshute named Tuilla helped load the carriage with the pine box containing Paco's body.

Tuilla was named for a nineteenth century ancestor, a Goshute leader with the same surname. He would've had no idea even if he hadn't been simple minded, that eventually Toole, Utah, would be named after his prominent ancestor, or that Tooele would become the location of the Dugway Proving Grounds.

More composed now, Kimama asked, "What happened to my Paco?"

"He was trying to prove that the Goshutes shouldn't have to go to war in Europe. He reached into his pocket for the federal document that proved 'is point. A soldier named Dial Kemmer thought he was pullin' a gun and shot'm"

"Did he suffer?"

"Jerry Barns, a lieutenant and the man in charge, who witnessed the killing said that he didn't, that he died instantly."

"That is good. He was a good man, and he didn't deserve to be in pain."

"Yeah."

"Paco *was* a good man . . . Why did this have to happen? Why?" Kimama asked.

"I don't know."

"What more can the white man do to us?"

"Hard to say."

"They've taken our land, our pride, our souls, many of our very lives."

"Kimama, life goes on, but perhaps someday they will pay for what they have done . . . perhaps in the afterlife."

"Perhaps, Chief Joe, perhaps."

"Are you takin' 'im out to Skull Valley to sink his body in a stream?"

"I'm not sure. Skull Valley is a long journey."

"Lieutenant Barns said you should take his body into Salt Lake for burial."

"Never. If I chose to bury him any way except the traditional Shoshone way, I'd have a ceremony among the Goshutes. But I'd never permit a ceremony and burial among the whites, never." She spit the words out with vehemence.

"So, you're handling his body according to ancient tradition?"

"I am, Chief Joe. So, good day to you."

"Good day."

The following day, Kimama decided not to take Paco to the traditional Goshute burial grounds in Skull Valley. It was too long a journey for little Sasquina. Instead, she took her husband's body to an out-of-the-way part of Deep Creek.

Mother and daughter dragged Paco's casket out of the carriage and positioned it on the banks of Deep Creek. They filled his clothing with rocks, kissed him on his lifeless, cold face and tumbled him into the creek. They cried for a spell before they could finish and take precautions that his body wouldn't float along on the current, even though it was weighted with rocks. They cut branches from a nearby spruce tree and sharpened the ends. They used the crudely fashioned stakes to drive down through Jake's clothing and into the creek bed. They used ten stakes to anchor him to the creek bed and then they headed back to the ranch, job completed.

After helping take care of her father's remains the traditional way, Sasquina went to her room and cried for the rest of the afternoon. Sasquina had never once considered that her father would just not "be." His death created an ache in her heart, an ache she feared would never go away.

Later that evening mother and daughter discussed what would be required of them to make a living. Neither knew much about cattle ranching, but they decided they were prepared to give it a try. "If we fail, we can go to my parents' place, live in that abandoned cabin and run sheep," Mary said.

"Yeah," Sasquina said.

"You'll have to put your painting aside; there will be no time for it."

Sasquina couldn't imagine a life spent not painting, but she answered in the affirmative. "Yeah, *Biá*, no painting," she said, huge tears welling up in her eyes.

The sight of those tears broke Kimama's heart. "I'm sorry, Sasquina, once we figure out how not to starve, you can start painting again."

"All right, *Biá*, all right. But if I can't paint I'll be sad."

"I know, I know."

Mother and daughter went off to bed, their problems largely unsettled. A pack of coyotes started in with their nocturnal, mournful howling. A jackrabbit exploded from behind a Joshua tree and dashed helter-skelter across the yard in front of the ranch house. The full moon had a ribbon of clouds stretched across its face. Then a microburst exploded downward onto a nearby hogback and churned up dust that settled on the ranch property. Then it poured rain, violently, unrelentingly for two solid hours. The desert soil was hungry and soaked up the moisture.

The next morning, Sasquina was surprised when her mother didn't bustle into her bedroom and shake her awake. That was something her mother had always done. Sasquina went looking for her and found her in her bed, stiff and dead. An old, chipped, white enamel cup sat on the nightstand. Sam took a sniff at the contents. It smelled awful, but she didn't know what it was, until she saw the bottle of strychnine next to the cup. Her apé had kept it around to poison coyotes that killed newborn calves and other ranch animals that were small and defenseless.

Sasquina was beyond shock. Her mother's face was twisted and discolored, awful to behold. It was more than Sasquina could endure.

She couldn't bear looking at her mother anymore, so she fled to her room to cry. She spent the remainder of the day crying. She even went so far as to consider going in there and taking a swig of that strychnine. But she thought of her need to paint, and gave that idea up. How could her *biá* have done such a thing?

Finally, after a miserable night, a night full of torment, she ventured back into her mother's room. She saw a bundle of papers on a nearby dresser. There was a note on the top of the bundle of papers that was tied with a twine. *I'm so sorry, Sasquina. I couldn't face a future without Paco.* The bundle of papers contained a deed to the house and surrounding cattle ranch, her birth certificate proving she was the offspring of Paco and Kimama Accawinna, and a bundle of assorted documents and private letters.

Sasquina placed them in a tin box and buried them near a creosote bush in their front yard. She knew enough about the white man's paper that she would need the deed to the house some day.

She saddled one of Paco's saddle horses and went to Ibapah and reported her mother's death to Chief Joe.

Chief Joe accompanied Sasquina back to the Accawinna homestead and the two of them loaded Kimama into a buckboard and took her to Deep Creek and submerged her next to her husband Paco in the same fashion he had been anchored to the creek bed.

They said very little during the solemn ceremony and they were soon driving the carriage back to the homestead.

"Sasquina," Chief Joe said, "a Mormon with many wives named Orson Briggs, who lives at the foothills of the Oquirrhs, north of here, will pick you up tomorrow. I sent Tuilla to bring him and pick you up. He'll adopt you as one of his own. He has so many wives and children that one more won't matter."

"I don't want to live with a white family," Sasquina said.

"Sorry, Sasquina. I'm afraid we don't have a choice. There is no one in these parts that can take on the burden of raising an extra child."

"So be it," Sasquina said, without shedding so much as one tear. She was all cried out.

The next afternoon a man shaped like a pumpkin with eyes that looked like raisins, and a great slobbery, tobacco-stained cavern for a mouth pulled up in a 1914 Mack flatbed truck. The flatbed had stakes and was rigged for hauling cattle. The truck was splattered with green cow manure and smelled foul.

She climbed in the front seat with him and they were off. She had never ridden in a horseless carriage and it was exciting, but at the same time she was fearful of riding off with the man who was to fill in as her father.

He put a huge, filthy hand high up on her thigh and introduced himself. "Hello there, Missy, the name's Briggs, Orson Briggs," he said.

"Hello, I am Sasquina Accawinna," she said, pulling his hand off her thigh.

He laughed at her. "Spunky little thing, eh?"

"I don't know about that, but I do know that I don't want your hand on my leg."

"Rightly so, young lady, rightly so. But not to fear, not to fear. I'm harmless. I'm a former bishop of an LDS ward over in Salt Lake. "

"Where are we goin'?"

"To my cattle ranch tucked up under the Oquirrhs."

"Are you adopting me? That's what Chief Joe said."

"I am, indeed. You'll move into one of my homes—I have three—and you will instantly be a part of a family of seven brothers and sixteen sisters."

"You mean to say one wife had all those kids?"

"No, no, heavens no. I have six wives. Two of them are living at the home you're going to. To 'go forth and multiply' is the will of the Lord."

"Which wife will be my *bia*?"

"Her name is Judith, and she shares the home with Bonnie. Between the two of them they have six children; you'll be the seventh living there in that home."

She was fearful when she asked this question, but she needed to know. "Do you live there?"

"No, I only visit there on occasion, to have . . . communion with those two dear wives. I know you'll miss my presence, but my cattle holdings and other commitments keep me on the run."

"I'll make do."

He laughed. "You Indian children have spirit," he said.

He dropped her off at her new home, introduced her to her adopted family, and then drove off, leaving her there to cope with her new environment.

She lived there two years before she saw Orson Briggs again. The only contact she and her instant family had had with Orson was a monthly Federal Reserve note drawn on a Federal Reserve Bank in Salt Lake. He sent them the rather smallish note each month for living expenses.

Her stepmother, Judith, was slightly over six feet tall and weighed nearly 300 pounds and she was shaped like a pear.

It took a little while, but Sasquina soon became comfortable with her new family. Her brothers and sisters seemed to accept her and the two women living in the house embraced her as their own and they teamed up as co-stepmothers. She tried forgetting about her biological parents for the time being. It made life bearable.

The house sat in the center of a small dairy farm and everybody worked, including two three-year-old children. It was a communal thing and required that everybody contribute in order to make it work. Sam's job was to go to the pasture morning and evening and herd the cows to the barn, then help milk them. She learned to squeeze the teats, starting the squeeze rhythmically at the top and transferring the squeeze sequentially down the fingers to the bottom, and stripping the udders of every drop of milk. Several other children in the brood were given the task of churning the milk into butter, buttermilk, and cream that were packaged neatly, along with the milk, for sale. Utahans came from far and near to the Briggs Dairy to purchase the dairy products. The Orson Briggs dairy generated a fairly substantial sum of money that went toward operating the household. The household managed quite nicely with Orson's monthly Federal Reserve notes generated from his cattle business, and with the income from the small dairy and its products. Further, the co-stepmothers and their brood had a vegetable garden, laying hens, pigs, and a couple beef cattle.

Sasquina attended school during the season and became a topnotch student. The school district had a new Model T school bus. The bus was mounted on an extended Model T frame and it had a twenty horse-power engine with a chain and sprocket drive. The student compartment itself was constructed of wood. It had inflatable tires in the front and solid tires in the rear, which made for a bumpy ride. The bus gathered twenty children from all around the district to attend a one-room schoolhouse in Wendover that serviced grades one through nine. She enjoyed school, but she missed painting. She asked her stepmothers from time to time if she could make a trip to Deep Creek near Ibapah and collect her art supplies.

"There is no time around here for painting and such folderol," she was told.

Then one day Orson Briggs came chugging into the yard in his cow-manure-splattered cattle truck and Sasquina's world was uprooted.

Everybody dashed toward Orson. His two wives seemed eager to see him. After all, they hadn't incubated children for two barren years. The children gathered about him because he always brought them candy. He hardly acknowledged his wives and he didn't give the children candy, or even so much as give anyone the time of day.

Instead, he went straight to Sasquina. "How are you doing, Sasquina?" he asked.

"Fine."

"Have you taken to farm life?"

"I have," Sasquina said, "and I want to thank you, sir, for givin' me a place to live. I don't know what I would've done—"

Orson didn't seem to hear the thank-you proffered him, because he was busy giving her a steady once-over with his eyes. "How old are you now, girl?"

"I just turned fourteen, sir" she said.

"Uh-huh. Well my, my, is that so, fourteen? This is nineteen eighteen, so you've been here four years now. I understand you're quite the scholar now, but that don't mean much, women should stay to home, cook, clean, make babies."

"Why'd you ask about my age, sir?"

"I can answer that by providing you with an old expression: 'If they're old enough to bleed they're old enough to—'" He decided it wouldn't be proper to complete the expression in front of Sasquina. After all, he didn't want to frighten her away. Besides, it wasn't a proper thing for a former LDS Bishop to be saying. He mentally upbraided himself. Sometimes he just said things that weren't in keeping with the tenets of the LDS Church.

"Sasquina, I am going to spend a couple nights here, visiting my loving wives, and on the third morning I am driving to a household I have over near Tremonton. A sad thing happened: One of my dear wives died and I'll be wanting you as a replacement. I'll want you to have your possessions ready three mornings hence, because you will be leaving with me." Having said that he slid an index finger down the channel between her budding breasts.

Her reaction was instantaneous. She slapped him a good one right across his fat face.

He blinked in amazement, and a red handprint blossomed on his cheek, but he still laughed. "Ah, a feisty one. I like spirited women. Be ready to go when I get back," he snapped as he departed.

That night Sasquina sneaked out of Orson Briggs farm house with just what she was wearing on her back. She walked through the night and managed to catch a ride on a buckboard with Tuilla, who happened to be traveling that dirt tract that night on his buckboard. Sasquina knew him from the old days. The old fellow dropped her off in Ibapah and she walked the rest of the way to Deep Creek. When she cleared the last hogback that looked down on the Accawinna Ranch she was surprised to see the place looked lived in. Smoke rose from the chimney that chilly February morning.

She burst in the kitchen unannounced and found an elderly lady stoking the coals in the kitchen range. The old gal was standing there in a pink nightgown and her silver hair reached nearly to her waist. She was a petite little thing with a waist so thin it looked unnatural. But the most noticeable feature was her eyes. They were a startling jade green that seemed to pierce right into one's soul. It was obvious she had once been very beautiful and was still very elegant.

"Who are you?" Sasquina asked.

"This cuts two ways, who are you?" the old woman returned.

"I'm the owner of this ranch and you shouldn't be here. I have the deed."

"I knew you'd return some day. Sasquina, about your parents, I am so sorry. You are Sasquina, aren't you?"

"I am Sasquina and I want you to leave."

"Sit down," the elderly lady said, "let's have coffee and talk."

"Talk? No. Get out. I am tired of getting kicked around by older people. I just escaped from a Mormon that wanted me for a wife. He was a fat, ugly ol' thing."

"Walk over to that window and look out and tell me what you see," the woman said.

Sasquina kicked a chair across the kitchen. "No, I want you off my property!" She pushed the old woman toward the door. The old lady resisted and was surprisingly strong for her age and size, but Sasquina finally shoved the old lady out onto the porch.

But once they arrived on the porch, Sasquina took a moment to look around. She hadn't done that when she walked up to the ranch house so intent had she been on seeing who was in her house and burning a fire in the kitchen. What she saw then was astonishing. There was a nicely tended garden, flowers everywhere, a picket fence around the ranch house, and freshly cut grass. There were cattle speckling the landscape, foraging on what grasses they could find in the sere landscape. The ranch yard was teeming with cats, dogs, chickens, a sow with six piglets at her teats, and a couple goats chewing the bark off the posts on a newly built horse corral.

Sasquina couldn't help it, her mouth popped open and she couldn't seem to shut it. "About that coffee," she finally managed to say.

"That's no way to treat an old lady," the tiny woman said, smoothing out her nightgown and going back through the door into the kitchen.

"Sorry," Sasquina said, "I just thought you were some beggar that'd moved in."

"We are, sorta, beggars. My name is Pearl Mower," the old lady said.

"Mower?"

"Yeah, Mower, it's a shortened Polish name. I can't even remember what it started out being before it got cut down to Mower, Mowerzanisky, or something like that. My parents were immigrants to this country and they shortened their surname when they arrived at Ellis Island. You can't imagine the jokes I've suffered over the years."

"Let's have coffee."

"Okay, Sasquina, you stay out here and look around. It'll only take me a few minutes."

In a few minutes the two ladies sat down to coffee.

"Make no mistake, this is my place," Sasquina said, "I have the deed hidden in a safe place."

"I don't doubt you," Pearl said.

"Why are you squattin' on my property?"

"Let me give you my background first. I was once a sporting girl and I worked at all sorts of bordellos across the United States. Then when I got too old for that line of work I became a madam out in San Francisco. I ran a house called Pearl's Pleasure Palace."

"That's sad."

"So, you do understand what I am telling you?"

"Yeah, how terrible. How could you?"

"I liked eating. Look, girl, I thought telling you the truth would be the best policy. I'm hoping we can form a partnership and I want to start it out based on trust."

"I doubt we can. I don't want to be in partnership with a . . . whore."

"You are the frank one, I'll say that for you," Pearl said.

"It's the way I am. What brought you here, to Deep Creek?"

"The city council in San Francisco passed an ordinance disallowing all sporting houses in all of San Francisco County. It was a cruel thing, turning an old lady out like that."

"Why are you here?"

"I stumbled on this deserted ranch on my way east to New Jersey, to see if any of my kin would take me in. I decided to squat. Chief Joe said he couldn't see any harm in squatting, just so I didn't damage anything, because he thought you might return some day. As you can see, I haven't damaged the place. In fact—"

"You're too old to have done all of this," Sasquina swept her hand across the nicely groomed ranch.

"Indeed, I am; I took on good help." She put two fingers to her mouth and blew a piercing whistle. Three Mexicans came trotting out of a newly built bunkhouse. They said their hellos, bowed politely, and went back to the bunkhouse.

"What in the world?" Sasquina asked.

"They are refugees from the Mexican Revolution."

"I see."

"Just briefly, it brought about the Mexican Constitution back in nineteen-seventeen. These three fellows were farmers before the revolution, so it hasn't been too difficult for them to adapt to ranching. They are here working for food and shelter. I haven't been able to pay them wages, but they aren't unhappy with the arrangement."

"Pearl, what you've done here is incredible. But working them so hard for just food and shelter seems wrong."

"Nah, Sasquina, they went into this thing with their eyes wide open. This is a good set-up for 'em. If they hadn't found this ranch they mighta starved."

"It looks like my father's cattle have doubled in number. I thought the original herd would be scattered everywhere, or stolen."

"As near as I can figure, I pulled in here two days after you were carted off by that Mormon."

"Really."

"I've heard if those polygamists get a blue veiner that nothing's safe that crosses their path."

"You've got that right. That ol' Mormon would couple with anything that has a heartbeat."

Pearl laughed, a roaring full-throated laugh. "Now I have a question. Didn't the U.S. come up with a law agin polygamy?"

"They did," Sasquina said, "but Mormons are still doin' it out in places where they won't be easily caught. Heck, actually, it's still goin' on in Salt Lake in some places, Briggs' wives told me."

"Did you run away from the polygamist?"

"I did."

"Well, I doubt he'll come after you. No doubt his many wives will keep him occupied. But if he does happen to come callin', I'll put Johnny Law on him."

"Right, that should make him lose his 'blue veiner.'"

Pearl laughed again. "Now let's talk about being partners on this here ranch. We need each other. And as you can see, I certainly have a stake in this operation." She pointed to the ranch and the grazing cattle. "I put most of my savings in this place, building that bunkhouse and what all. I took a gamble."

"Okay. We can be partners. But you need to understand one thing right off."

"And that would be?"

"If we form a partnership, I'm the boss, the only boss. There can only be one boss."

"Fair enough. I'm all ears."

"I'm not interested in what your plans are. After I tell you my plan, you might think it's a crazy notion, but if you stay patient I'll explain my reasoning behind it." Sasquina had been thinking about going to Salt Lake for some time, so this plan had already been partially worked out in her mind.

"I'm listenin'"

The two women walked back to the kitchen. They went back in to rustle up some breakfast.

The three Mexicans came back out of curiosity, they wanted to know who the stranger was, so they politely slipped into the kitchen. The pungent odor of hard working, unwashed bodies, and cigarillo smoke trailed in with them.

"Sit down, boys, meet the owner of this ranch and your new boss," Pearl said.

Sam shook each of their hands. "Who did all the work out there?" she asked the Mexicans.

"We all did our share, *señora*," a small, prunish-looking man said. "I am Don Carlos and this fellow is Juan Lopez"—he pointed to one of the other men, who was strikingly handsome—"and this old fellow is Jesus Rodriquez."

"Sit down, gentleman. I have a proposal."

They sat at the table and Pearl put cups in front of them and poured coffee.

"I want to sell this ranch and move to Salt Lake," Sasquina said, taking a sip of coffee.

"What about us?" Carlos asked, "If you do that we will have no place to go."

"Pearl, are these men honest? I know they're hard workers."

"They are."

"Are you an honest woman?"

"I am."

"Are they legal citizens of the U.S.?" She pointed to the three Mexicans.

"No, not exactly, they—"

"Well, if we form a partnership, I want them to take the steps to become legal citizens . . . that's the first thing."

"Gotcha," Pearl said.

"*Si, señora*," Carlos said.

"Further, I'll want you three to learn better English."

"Why?" Pearl asked.

"Because we are going to be living in Salt Lake, and I'll want them to be able to talk to and be understood by the people in Salt Lake."

"*Si, señora*," Carlos said again.

"Well, good, now that that is understood. Do you want to move to Salt Lake and take a crack at this thing I have in mind?"

"But why sell this little ranch? We have put it in such nice condition," Pearl asked, lighting a cigarette.

"I have to. I want to pursue a career in landscape portraiture."

"How can we make a living doing that?" Pearl asked.

"Here is how it will be done. We will buy a house up in Salt Lake, then use the remainder of the money to buy an art supply business. Don, Juan, and Jesus will run the business, that's why I want you men to speak English well, and Pearl, you will run the house and keep the books for the home and the business. I'll paint; that's all I'll do, paint. We will all live in the house, form a corporation, and put our assets in a joint account that can't be drawn upon unless there are five signatures."

"Go on," Lucy said.

"I own fifty percent of the corporation, Pearl owns twenty, and the remaining three have ten percent apiece."

"I'm for it," Pearl said. "I've sunk nearly a thousand dollars in this ranch. I figure I can get that back easy enough. I'm willing to give it try . . . if nothing else I'll have a roof over my head. What about you fellows?" She looked at the three Mexicans.

"*Si, señora*, we go to Salt Lake." Don Carlos said, speaking for the group. They all nodded.

"Well, there you go," Sasquina said, "it's a done deal. We'll sell this ranch, then move to Salt Lake, find a place to buy big enough for all of us, we'll draw up a contract, and buy the art business. Then later on, we'll adjust our business dealings as needed."

"Why are you taking us on as partners, when you hardly know us?" Pearl asked.

"I don't know anybody else, really. I am taking a risk on you four, hoping you won't disappoint me. I need to set it up so that I have plenty of spare time to paint, and paint, and paint. I am praying the art business will work for us, provide enough money for food and other necessities. I need companions, partners, people around me. Besides, looking out over this ranch tells me what I need to know about you people."

"When do we do this?" Pearl asked.

"Right now, " Sam said.

"We won't disappoint you," Carlos said, "we will be good shopkeepers. We will sell mucho art . . . art brushes for you, *señora*."

"Here's a few more things you four should know. I'm not going to help with the art supply business and you're going to sell me supplies wholesale. I'm going to paint landscape portraits until my fingers bleed. I am a landscape artist and I haven't sat in front of an easel for two years. The second item, when the pictures start to sell, and they will start to sell, we will share in those profits as well."

"Are you good?" Pearl asked, sounding a bit doubtful that just a slip of a girl could paint well enough to make money at it.

To answer Pearl's pointed question, Sasquina slid a hidden panel back in the rear of a closet and pulled out her collection of landscape paintings that had been stored there in leather fold-over portfolios. Sam pulled the portraits out and showed Pearl the one of Ibapah Peak.

"My God," Pearl said, "who would have thought?"

The Mexicans just stared, their mouths agape.

"It's *muy bonito, señora, muy bonito*," Don Carlos said.

"One last thing. If any one of you four disappoint me in any way, you'll be sent packing. Don't steal from me, don't lie to me, don't drink, don't quarrel. If you do, the remaining shareholders will buy you out, and you're gone, period."

Pearl took a minute to explain to the Mexicans what Sasquina had just said. When they finally understood, they looked at Sasquina with a sort of grudging admiration, but they agreed to the terms.

"What do you think this ranch is worth?" Pearl asked.

"Quite a lot. My apé told me it was worth fifteen thousand, and that was before you four made all of these improvements." She went to the kitchen window and ran her eyes over the spread.

"Who is *apé*?" Pearl asked, squinting her eyes and shaking her head.

"Daddy, that was my Daddy, the one the whites killed."

"Gotcha."

"Pearl, do you think that will be enough money?"

"Yeah, that should be plenty to buy a nice home and set up an art supply business."

"Good," Sasquina said. "Hopefully, when we move there we can keep those Salt Lake polygamists away from us."

"I don't think I have anything to worry about, I just turned seventy," Lucy said, laughing. "But you on the other hand?"

The Mexicans only partially understood what had been said, but they still joined in on the laugher, the first the group had shared together.

"That's funny, *señoras*," one said, laughing from the belly.

"Uh, what makes you think we can even sell this ranch?" Pearl asked.

"There are two Goshute who have ranches bordering ours. Both offered to buy my father out in order to make their ranches larger. Neither can pay cash, but both could get a loan in Salt Lake."

"Okay, I suggest we play them off agin each other to get the price up," Pearl said.

"Pearl," Sasquina said, "I want you to handle the sale. You have experience with such things, don't you? You can be the boss of this part of it."

"Yeah, I've sold a couple pieces of property in my day. So, let's get to work and sell this place . . . you can all help."

Five years later, at the ripe old age of nineteen, Sasquina walked out of her home on one of the fashionable Salt Lake City avenues. She was accompanied by Pearl Mower, now seventy-five years old, head housekeeper and accountant. A taxi waited for them at the curb. They were dressed elegantly because Sasquina was having her first art showing down on 21st South and 13th East. A brand spanking new art gallery had just opened there named The Golden Spike. The Golden Spike was destined to get in financial trouble three years later and re-emerge in Corrine, Utah. Regardless, The Golden Spike played a major role in Sasquina's ascension as a great landscape artist.

The three Mexican painting supply shopkeepers met the two ladies in the entrance and they went in together to see which, if any, of Sasquina's portraits would sell.

Sasquina leaned in and whispered to the Mexicans, "What do you three like better, farming or being president, vice-president, and head accountant of Little Sasquina's Paints and Art Supplies?"

"We like living and working in the art world, *señora*. Thank you so much for givin' us work," Don Carlos said.

"Don't mention it. Hard work has put you where you are."

The Mexicans, in fact, had come up in the world. They were legal American citizens, they spoke serviceable English, and they had gone in together and bought a nice little house in Holiday, a Salt Lake suburb "We are settled into our new home, *señora*; you must pay us a visit."

"I'll do that."

"Sasquina," Lucy said, "don't look now, but the governor, Charles Mabey, is walking up the walk. Those landscapes you've been selling all over the world have brought him in for a look-see."

"Quick, before he and his bride get here. Answer this, are you happy here in Salt Lake?"

"I've never been happier. Thank you, Sasquina. That day you caught me and these three Mexicans squatting on your ranch," she pointed to them, "well, I thought it was all over for the four of us. If you'd run us off I don't know what would become of us."

"And does your growing bank account please you?"

"Yeah, I just wish I wasn't so old. I really would like to stick around a while to spend it all."

"Smile big, here comes the governor, his wife, the city mayor, and several Salt Lake City councilmen. Smile big."

Sasquina, Pearl, and the three Mexicans, all dressed to the nines, smiled big.

The showing was a rousing success, and five of her portraits sold and brought a sizable amount of money. Governor Mabey, in fact, bought a landscape of the Waterpocket Fold that Sasquina painted while visiting a region in south central Utah that was soon, in 1937, to be set aside by Congress as Capitol Reefs National Park.

Nearly one hundred years later, seven of Sasquina Accawinna's landscape portraits were displayed at The Golden Spike, an art show up in Northern Utah at Corrine. The art show featured Utah art from 1825 through 1925.

Sasquina's landscape portrait of Ibapah Peak and four others painted near Ibapah were prominently on display. But there were two other curious paintings on display, not landscapes at all. A powerful, macabre portrait of an Indian woman slumped over in bed, dead of strychnine poisoning. Her face was horribly contorted from the ravishes of the poison. The other portrait was of a dead Indian man, staked through his clothing to the bottom of a streambed. The Indian's face was distorted by the water; it looked kind of like a Picasso.

Years later those macabre portraits would end up in the Guggenheim in New York. Dozens of Sasquina's landscape portraits ended up adorning the walls of the world's most renowned museums.

The art enthusiasts there at Corrine couldn't figure out why the late, great landscape artist, Sasquina Accawinna had painted the portraits of dead Indians. The stark, gritty reality on display in those portraits were a slap to the kisser for the art enthusiast. A smattering of hoity-toity art aficionados retired to their penthouses up in Park City and over in Deer Valley, sipped expensive Champagne, nibbled at their Brie and tried to rationalize why Sasquina would paint those disturbing portraits. To them, it seemed so . . . unseemly. But there was no denying it—that long-dead Indian maiden could really paint.

MARKING

My name is Allison Meldvedt and during my senior year at the Barstow School located on the old State Line Road in Kansas City, Missouri, I discovered I might be a lesbian. This shocker came to me during my twenty-second year—late in life, I've always thought, to discover I wasn't "normal." If I could have ignored these urgings to hit on the same sex, I could have avoided a lot of problems down the road.

Barstow is one of America's top coed finishing schools, and the alma mater for several celebrities: Bess Truman, a former first lady; James Metzer, a politician and national security expert; Jean Harlow, a film actress; and Eldar Djanirov, a jazz pianist. Dear old Barstow simply reeks of tradition and respectability.

Anyway, I was shocked when I discovered I liked hitting on other women. My discovery began innocently enough one night when my roommate, also a senior, and I decided to share a kiss, just for a lark . . . and here all along I'd always thought same-sex kisses were barf city. But the trouble is, the kiss was nice and it led to ninety minutes of lovemaking in our dorm room behind a locked door—students from adjoining rooms regularly walked in without knocking. I remember we left the television playing while we messed around. We were a captive audience to a debate between Presidential Candidates Barack Obama and John McCain. Neither of us dared to get up and turn the thing off for fear the mood would be spoiled.

With that kiss, I discovered pleasures that I hadn't known existed. I'd tried sex with men, but the thing that happened between me and Candace Pope was so much better that there just wasn't any comparison. Her skin was soft and wonderful to the touch, and she responded to me with loving gusto. The loving she delivered was not like the rutting, maladroit fumbling I'd suffered at the hands of several males there at Barstow. It was almost like we consumed each other.

We did things to each other that are simply unspeakable in polite company—I think. For example, she fisted me, if you get my drift and brought me to multiple orgasms. It was off the chain. Then, feeling that turnabout was fair play, I tried to offer her the same treatment, but I failed because of dimensional problems. This is the last I'll talk about the details because it makes most people uneasy. Hell, in retrospect, it makes me uneasy.

I just wanted to expose the startling transformation that came over me on that night two weeks ago, and a mere two days before our graduation from dear old Barstow.

The next morning we climbed out of our beds and we couldn't look at each other. That was sad, I thought, telling myself we really hadn't done anything beyond the pale. After all, one out of ten people say they're gay and probably performing similar acts daily. No doubt good old Barstow itself had probably had its share of lesbians over the years, considering it has had plenty of time to accumulate special lovers like us; Barstow has been around dating back to 1884, and was founded by Mary Louise Barstow.

Anyway, regardless of all my efforts to assure myself it was all right and that there had been others who'd gone before me, and others that would come after, I was still stricken with guilt. I suppose it's just human nature. The guilt didn't stop me, though, from going with this new lifestyle; I was determined to go ahead with it and somehow learn to relax with it.

It took hours before Candace and I sat down and discussed what had gone on the night before. I felt the need to end the guilt-induced freeze up, so after a short reading session I snapped the book shut, turned off Fox News playing a sound bite of Hillary Clinton at the 2008 Iowa Presidential Caucus, and said, "Goddamnit it, Candace, let's talk."

"Well, yeah."

"You fisted me."

"I know."

"And I liked it—really liked it."

"I figured you must have, considering the gasping and moaning."

"Do you love me?"

"Yeah, I do."

"I think I love you, too."

"It complicates our lives."

"Tell me about it."

"Allison, we just might be lesbians."

"Duh. We got naked and had sex. You needn't draw me a diagram."

"It'll complicate our lives."

"You think? I Googled what being gay in America is like."

"And?"

"And, well, if we decide to be life partners, we'll suffer social, political, religious, legal, and economic discrimination."

"Is that all?" she asked, laughing.

"Funny."

She ignored that. "You'll have to tell your new flame, Sam Peterson, to get lost."

"No problem, our relationship sucked from the get-go."

"I figured as much."

"And you'll have to tell the entire men's Lacrosse team to look for their thrills elsewhere," I said, laughing.

"Ha-ha, you're a million laughs." Her face turned serious. "Uh, did you have any idea, you know, about yourself?"

"Kind of, I guess. There were a few clues. Men have just never done it for me; I've always thought they were grody. But I always thought I'd get over myself and begin liking them properly."

"Well, I think they are grody, grody to the max, in fact, and I'm serious," Candace said, looking in the mirror as she combed out her full head of blond hair. Candace was tall, long-limbed, and beautiful, with classic features. Actually, I can't imagine what she saw in me. I'm short, dark-complexioned, slightly overweight, and not what one would consider beautiful. Can it be true that opposites attract?

"What do you mean?" I asked. "Do you mean you sensed you were wired differently early on?"

"Yeah. I had a thing for a young, gorgeous female English teacher in high school back in Boston."

Carol Pennington burst into our dorm room. Her room was just across the hall. "Girls, guess what?" she asked.

"Let me guess, you were recently betrothed to a twelve-year-old Mongoloid idiot named Bubba?" Candace asked. It wasn't that Candace disliked Carol, speaking to her like that, it was just that nearly everybody on our floor there at the dorm had taken to throwing insults around—it was a sort of game.

"I'm so sure," Carol snapped back, glaring at Candace. Carol's hair was a fright and she was parading around in a tattered nightgown.

"What's the news, Carol?" I asked, deciding Carol had had enough insults hurled at her, at least for that day. "Don't you have to start putting on your face to be ready to graduate?"

"I'm working at it and trying to get especially beautiful because Sean Hawkins asked me to attend graduation with him and then go out to a nightclub. I am so excited I think I'm going to wet my pants."

"Congratulations, Carol," I said.

Carol looked to Candace for her blessings as well. Sean Hawkins lived in a nearby dormitory and, admittedly, he was cute. "Well?" she asked, looking at Candace.

"Congratulations Carol," Candace said. "Now take a hike; Allison and I were having a private conversation."

"You're such a rude be-atch," she said, leaving in a huff.

Candace stood staring at me, transfixing me with her gorgeous set of green eyes. Then Mother Nature took over and there was no turning it aside. I felt a tingling in my southern regions. So I walked over, got on my tippy-toes and kissed her full on the mouth. She seemed to enjoy it. Her breath smelled like Crest toothpaste, but before I got to her mouth I got a whiff of her Lancome Poeme perfume—it was intoxicating . . . Candace was intoxicating. So when it was over I tried to guide her toward the bed.

"Not now," she said, resisting my advance. "Let's talk this thing over. We have got ourselves a situation here. Let's go to our graduation today and then tonight when Carol is in Sean's arms you can be in mine. Besides, the door is unlocked."

"Right," I said, "let's talk it over." I didn't want to just talk it over, I wanted more, but I supposed it was for the best.

And talk we did, for a solid hour. In the end we decided it would be all right to be lovers, life-partners if you will. By hooking up in such a way we were both certain that mutual love would eventually come, if we just gave it a chance. We were on such a high.

We decided to live together in Boston. Candace said that we should be able to find work in Boston, using our degrees from Barstow, powerful tools in the employment market. She said she had enough money to carry us until we found work.

Candace comes from a privileged background and I come from one bordering on poverty. I got into Barstow with top grades from high school, an academic scholarship, and a Pell Grant. Candace's parents paid her way. They were both attorneys-at-law with humongous stock options in a huge law firm there in Boston, and my parents owned and operated a dilapidated beer joint on the Tamiami Trail, a highway connecting Fort Myers, Florida, with Miami. My parents drink their own sales product regularly and are mostly too drunk to make their little bar named Bug-eyed Betty's, pay. Their earnings barely cover the overhead. I love them and I wished they'd stop drinking so much, but there's not much I can do to make it happen.

Candace suggested I call my parents in Fort Myers and tell them I was moving to Boston. I was happy to, not really caring to go home. I'd always intended to make my own way in the world. So, it was all set. Our lives together would be off the chain. We thought it best to keep it on the QT for right now, though. The modern-day world had accepted same-sex couples more so than any other time in history, but we were reluctant to out ourselves.

Homosexuality was still looked on askance by Christian groups, and I'm sure that my parents would've been against it, totally unsympathetic. I did a little research on it and discovered that homosexuality was considered a mental disorder up until nineteen seventy-two, when the American Psychiatric Association removed it from their list, but that didn't mean society was opening their arms wide to special lovers.

After a short time I broke the silence. "What about adopting children?" I asked.

"Whoa, whoa, slow down. We're not even ready to come out of the closet. Maybe someday."

I thought about that for a minute and then my mind bounded off into another direction, searching for a diversion. Knowing who we were, it was fairly obvious that I'd fulfill the roll of female/mother, so I was thinking I wanted a baby. But Candace put the kibosh to that. It was disappointing, but I decided she was right, that we should wait. "Hey, if I can't have my baby right away, I have another request."

"And that would be?"

"You know that I've always wanted to go to Utah, the Beehive State?"

"Yeah, but I have no clue why," Candace said, smoothing out the bedspread on her bed she'd just finished making. "Why not the Riviera, the south of France, Monte Carlo, the Hamptons? You get all bothered about wanting to visit Utah. Isn't it just a desert?"

"No, they've got canyonlands, alpine forest, prairie land, and, of course, desert."

"Wow, thanks for the travelogue," Candace said, sarcasm dripping.

I ignored her. "As soon as we graduate, can we visit Utah and celebrate our newly formed life partnership? I've studied Utah for years and I want to explore the backcountry, do some backpacking. Are you up for that?" I looked at her with wide-eyed anticipation. "Please? Pretty please? I have two frequent flyers tickets and just enough cash to swing it."

Candace looked less than pleased at the prospect of tramping about Utah's backcountry, but she managed a little smile. "I can't say that I'm much into backpacking into the backcountry. Isn't there bugs and shit?"

"Please! A little bug can't hurt you."

It took a little while, but she finally changed her mind; I could see it in her face. "Oh, all right, but just for you."

"Yippee, at long last I get to see Utah—the land of Brigham Young."

Candace shook her head and pursed her lips. "You realize that this thing with Utah is some weird shit? Why Utah?"

"I can't really say. To me there is a mystique about it, or maybe it's the name. I'll make the arrangements for us to fly to Salt Lake City, rent a Jeep and head to the backcountry. I think we should drive down to the southern part of the state to Zion National Park. You'll love it."

"Are there wild animals that like eating people?"

"Don't be a boob. Most of the wild critters have been wiped out. We'll be safe, and we'll have a great 'honeymoon' in Zion National Park."

"All right," Candace said, reluctantly.

"It can be a beginning for us. Who knows, maybe someday we'll spend all of our vacations in the wild. We'll become . . . naturalists."

"Sheesh," Candace said.

We flew into Salt Lake City, Utah, a week later, rented a Jeep Grand Cherokee and headed to State Street. We drove south on State and pulled into the Big 5 Sporting Goods in Murray. We bought a tent, backpacks, utensils, a Coleman Lantern and everything else we needed for the back country. Then we hopped on I-15 and continued south toward Zion National Park. I was driving, so I stopped at an Eagles Landing Chevron station in Scipio.

"Why are you stopping here? We have plenty of gas," Candace asked.

"I just think it's a good idea to always have a full tank," I said, "in case we decide to drive off-road and explore."

"Sheesh," she said.

After we topped off the tank we sat for a minute to make plans. But actually we stopped to steal a kiss or two and cop a feel. "Let's roll, Zion National Park calls," Candace said, rolling her eyes.

"You aren't going to ruin this for me, are you?" I asked, miffed a bit, I admit, by her tone.

"I hadn't intended to."

"Well, please don't, I've looked forward to this trip since I was a little girl. I've never been in the American West and I think this is cool."

"Sorry, girlfriend, I forgot myself."

"Now take this cute little town, Scipio, for instance. I know a little bit about its history. You want to know anything about where we are?"

"Yeah, why not, tell me," she said, being polite.

"It's part of America's heritage."

"Okay, okay, tell me about Scipio."

"The early names for Scipio were Round Valley and Craball. It had a population of two-ninety, as of the two thousand census. It became a town in eighteen fifty-nine and it sits in the middle of a round valley. The first industry here was cattle ranching. Now it's selling high-priced gasoline to tourists like us. The town is named for Scipio Kenner. And—"

"Wow. Listen, Allison, what you're saying is neat, and you are so cute tellin' it, but I suppose that's all I need to know about Scipio. Can we talk about something else? We, that's all two of us, can stay happy and talk about something else, can't we?"

"Okay, like what?"

"I don't know, it's your show today." She continued looking me over with those big green eyes, looking into my soul, it seemed. Then she leaned over and kissed me, a deep, passionate kiss. "You're cute as can be over this, and you really do care about this tiny town and all the other tiny little towns here in Utah, don't you?"

"Yeah, I do, and I want to explore all of them, plus the backcountry." I looked at her after saying that. "I wish you genuinely shared my enthusiasm for exploration, for our heritage."

"I'm trying, cutie, trying hard. Tell you what, why don't we drive down I-15 a little ways, then let's take a dirt road and drive back into the backcountry and get into some camping? We can set up our tent and the whole nine yards. We don't need to drive all the way to Zion National Park today, do we? We just had a long flight."

"Really, you want to do that?" I was surprised because we had planned on staying in a motel in Cedar City for that first night.

"Yeah. We're going to backpack and camp in Zion National Park, so we might just as well get a feel for how it's done."

"Yeah," I shouted, pulling out onto I-15.

"After we set up camp we can start in on the case of beer we bought in Salt Lake City."

"Totally."

"Then, after we get shitfaced, who knows what could happen." She winked at me. The very idea of making love put us on a high. We laughed until we were giddy.

In the end, we decided to drive farther than originally planned to find a place to camp. We decided to get closer to Zion National Park. Then we wouldn't have to drive so far the next day and we could get into the backpacking at the Park even earlier.

When we arrived in Cedar City, we got off onto the wrong road, ending at a monument commemorating the Mountain Meadows Massacre that occurred in 1857. According to the monument, the Faincher-Baker immigrant wagon train that camped in an opening below on that date had been massacred by Mormon pioneers and Piute Indians—120 men, women, and children had been slaughtered. The kicker was that Brigham Young might have given the orders.

"How awful," Candace said, snuggling down into her jacket; evening was coming and it was getting a little chilly. "I can almost hear their screams."

A chill ran along my spine. "Me, too," I said.

"Let's get outta here."

Twenty minutes later we got the Jeep hopelessly stuck in the muddy ruts of a dirt road. We had pulled off the highway and driven back in to some out-of-the-way ranching country. It was a wet, murky place and smelled of mud and humus.

Not long after that a pack of coyotes began howling. We knew they were coyotes because we caught a glimpse of one running across a hill above us just before it went totally dark. Their eerie howls gave me the creeps and I'm sure Candace suffered in the same way. We sat there petrified for a while, sipping on our beer, and before we knew it, it was as dark as the inside of a cow. Then we really did get scared, scared shitless.

"Like, oh my God, are we going to be eaten?" Candace asked, trying to speak between little gasps and sobs.

"No, I don't think so," I said, joining in with a little blubbering of my own.

We sat there in the truck and cried like babies. "We're a couple 'fraidy cats." I said, "Let's stop and think about this and be realistic. They can't get to us in this Jeep."

"How do you know?"

"I just know."

"What if they come and knock out a window and hop in here?"

"That's unlikely," I said.

"What if nobody shows up to rescue us and we end up having to walk out of here to find food? They could get at us then."

"That's not gonna happen."

Candace started blubbering again, until I thought up a totally radical scheme that just might keep us safe from the coyotes. Hey, we were scared silly and we needed a plan, any plan. "I've got it!" I said. "Have you ever heard of marking?"

"Marking?" Candace asked.

"Marking, you know, staking out territory? Wild animals are territorial and they pee on stuff to keep other animals away. We could do that. I read about it in a zoology class at Barstow."

"Pee on stuff?" Candace said, incredulous. "I'm so sure."

"Yeah, let's pee a ring around this Jeep. It will keep the coyotes away. We've got all that beer."

"Sounds imbecilic. It can't work."

"I'm not sure it will work, but it can't hurt. We're gonna drink this beer and we're going to have to pee anyway, so why not do it in a circle? Do you have a better plan?"

"I think you're out of your mind, but I suppose I'll go along with it. It'll give us something to tell our grandchildren."

"Grandchildren? Us? Okay, let's get to peeing," I said, popping the lid on a Coors Beer.

It took hours, but we finally managed to pee a ring around the Jeep. Once we got the ring completed, we passed out . . . too much beer. And before we knew it, it was daylight, and we both popped awake and felt like shit.

"I read that coyotes more or less disappear in the daytime. I think it'll be safe to go for help."

"Totally," Candace agreed. "And let me suggest you step lightly when you get out of the Jeep . . . there's no tellin' what a gal could get on the soles of her shoes."

I laughed. We hoofed it back to Highway 18; it was a short trip. We didn't bother taking our gear along.

We got lucky because an old truck was coming along the highway, so we flagged it down. A gnarly old rancher stepped from his truck and looked us over. He had on a battered, sweat-stained hat and a tattered denim shirt and jeans. He looked as if a lifetime of hard work had beaten him down. "Are you girls in trouble?" he asked.

"Our rental Jeep is stuck in the mud," Candace said. "Do you suppose you could pull us out?"

"I suppose, hop in," he said.

We hopped in his truck and he drove us back in to where our Jeep was stuck. The rancher stepped out of his truck, and looked over the situation. "Yeah, this old truck can pull you out. But I have to ask, what're you doing here? This is my private property."

"Sorry sir, we didn't know we were trespassing," I said. "It was dark when we drove in."

"We were looking for a place to camp," Candace said.

"Darned queer place to be camping," he said. "It's just a bog."

We let him know that we understood and that we were sorry, and that seemed to calm him.

"Say," he said, "you ladies don't look so hot this morning, and you both smell like a brewery."

"We drank beer and marked our territory to keep from g'ttin' eaten by those horrible coyotes," I said.

"We peed a ring around our Jeep," Candace added, not mincing her words.

"Say what?" he asked. "Why would you do such a thing? I've been to a county fair and three goat ropes, but I have never heard tell of such a thing." He laughed until we thought he was going to blow his beets. It pissed us off.

"What would you have done?" I asked.

"I wouldn't have peed a ring around myself," he said, gasping and snorting for breath, between the guffaws. "You just sat in the Jeep drinking beer all night and got out and tinkled a ring around the rental?"

"Yeah," I said.

"You were afraid the coyotes were going to eat you?"

"Well, yeah," I said.

"Wait'll I tell Martha about this one," he said, wiping his eyes. "Coyotes have rarely been known to attack people, and there certainly isn't any way they could have gotten into the Jeep to get at you, even if they'd wanted to. They don't walk around with Slim Jims, you know."

He approached the Jeep with his chain, taking care to do a little hop when he got to the area were he figured the pee ring must have been laid down. We both noticed that and giggled. He just snorted in disapproval of our twittering. He pulled our Jeep out without much effort and we made our way back to Highway 18. We were both mad as hell at the old coot, even if he had pulled us out.

We ended up in St. George, Utah, only to find that we were too far south of Zion's. We bought more gas at a Maverik Country Store and headed back north toward Zion's. It was way hot there in St. George. Little beads of sweat trickled down between my boobs, even though the Jeep's air conditioner was on full blast. I noticed the Mormon Temple off in the background and the community itself was shoved up against huge red cliffs with giant red boulders that had broken loose and tumbled to a rest at the bottom, boulders as big as houses.

The little town was sweet, I thought it might be a cool place to live. I started getting ideas. I loved the place, it was splattered with greenery and flower gardens, and everything looked sparkling clean.

When we got to the turnoff at Hurricane that would have taken us in to Zion's, I had second thoughts about continuing on with the backpacking trip.

"Candace, let's not go into Zion's," I said. "I know you really aren't up for it, and I've changed my mind."

"Hey, girlfriend, I thought you were really up for this?"

"I use to be, but not now. Candace, I love you, I really do . . . and God knows I appreciate you agreeing to this, even though you just aren't the outdoor type. It was sweet of you."

"And?"

"And, I don't want to drag you in there after all. I can always use the camping equipment at a later time."

"Why do I think there is more?"

"Well, there is more. I'm not comfortable being gay. I'm sorry."

Tears welled up in her eyes. "I had a feeling this was going to happen. You really aren't one of us, are you?"

A Ford Pickup, pulling a four-horse trailer full of horses, went whizzing by us and cut into the lane in front of us, nearly taking the front end off the Jeep. I blasted the horn at him and called him a "stupid, shit-kickin' asshole." Candace laughed at that and I ended up joining in with her. We laughed long and hard, what the heck? Hey, the guy probably didn't even realize what he'd done.

I answered Candace's question, the one she'd asked before the near accident, feeling stupid about my answer. "I suppose I am not one of your sort," I said, ". . . but if I was, you'd be my first choice as a life-partner."

"I love you, girlfriend . . . I've enjoyed sharing my love with you."

"It has been exciting."

"What now?"

"You go back to Boston and find a wonderful replacement for me."

"I will."

"And I am going back to my parents' house in Florida and take a job at Bug-eyed Betty's, just long enough to make airfare back to Utah."

"You're shittin' me."

"I wouldn't shit you. I'm going to move to St. George and use my degree from dear old Barstow to get a good job. Surely some business there would be interested in taking on a girl who's a graduate from one of the top finishing schools in the country."

Ten years have passed since that aborted camping trip to Utah. I did get a good job in St. George at a dentist's office. DDS Carl Bradley's office, in fact. I ended up marrying Carl. Now I live in a beautiful home nestled in the red cliffs overlooking St. George, Utah. My husband, DDS Carl Bradley is a city councilman, a loyal member of the Moose Club, a volunteer for the Chamber of Commerce, and a devoted fly fisherman. He's the sweetest guy, a real catch, and a pillar of the community. I don't know what I'd do without him.

We have two little girls, Bonnie and Connie. I'm a fulltime housekeeper and a member of the PTA. When we entertain, I'm the perfect hostess, the polished little wife who's a graduate of Barstow. I don't say stuff like "tubular" anymore, or "barf me out," stuff like that. I try not to swear so much; it's not in keeping with the role of respectable dentist's wife or mother.

Candace lives in Boston. She's an executive secretary for Cornstyne Tattel Carawitch, attorneys at law. She has a live in girlfriend, a gal she has been with for nearly eight years. She continues, year after year, hoping that state lawmakers will pass legislation making it legal for her to get married in the state of Massachusetts, but the wheels of government turn slowly. We keep up a continual correspondence, Candace and I. I still love her . . . as a girl friend, not a girlfriend, if you get my drift.

I'm happy living here in the West. I love being a part of the vibrant, up-and-coming beehive state, Utah that takes its name, incidentally, from the Ute Indians, Ute meaning "people of the mountains." I, too, am a person of the mountains, that is, when Carl and I go north to backpack in the Uintahs or along the Wasatch Front.

THE END